Child
ABUSE

Opposing Viewpoints®

Other Books of Related Interest

Child
ABUSE
Opposing Viewpoints®

Louise I. Gerdes, *Book Editor*

Daniel Leone, *President*
Bonnie Szumski, *Publisher*
Scott Barbour, *Managing Editor*
Helen Cothran, *Senior Editor*

OPPOSING
VIEWPOINTS®
SERIES

GREENHAVEN
PRESS®

THOMSON
———— ✳ ————
GALE

San Diego • Detroit • New York • San Francisco • Cleveland
New Haven, Conn. • Waterville, Maine • London • Munich

THOMSON
GALE

LIBRARY OF CONGRESS CATALOGING-IN-PUBLICATION DATA

Child abuse : opposing viewpoints / Louise I. Gerdes, book editor.
   p. cm. — (Opposing viewpoints series)
Includes bibliographical references and index.
ISBN 0-7377-1674-6 (pbk. : alk. paper) — ISBN 0-7377-1673-8 (lib. : alk. paper)
   1. Child abuse—United States. 2. Child abuse—Investigation—United States.
3. Child molesters—United States. I. Gerdes, Louise I. II. Opposing viewpoints
series (Unnumbered)
HV6626.52 .C554 2003
362.76'0973—dc21
                                                         2002043083

Printed in the United States of America

"Congress shall make no law...abridging the freedom of speech, or of the press."

First Amendment to the U.S. Constitution

The basic foundation of our democracy is the First Amendment guarantee of freedom of expression. The Opposing Viewpoints Series is dedicated to the concept of this basic freedom and the idea that it is more important to practice it than to enshrine it.

Contents

Chapter 3: How Should the Legal System Combat Child Sexual Exploitation?

Chapter 4: How Can Child Abuse Be Reduced?

Why Consider
Opposing Viewpoints?

*"The only way in which a human being can make some
approach to knowing the whole of a subject is by hearing
what can be said about it by persons of every variety of
opinion and studying all modes in which it can be looked
at by every character of mind. No wise man ever
acquired his wisdom in any mode but this."*

John Stuart Mill

In our media-intensive culture it is not difficult to find differing opinions. Thousands of newspapers and magazines
and dozens of radio and television talk shows resound with
differing points of view. The difficulty lies in deciding which
opinion to agree with and which "experts" seem the most
credible. The more inundated we become with differing
opinions and claims, the more essential it is to hone critical
reading and thinking skills to evaluate these ideas. Opposing
Viewpoints books address this problem directly by presenting stimulating debates that can be used to enhance and
teach these skills. The varied opinions contained in each
book examine many different aspects of a single issue. While
examining these conveniently edited opposing views, readers
can develop critical thinking skills such as the ability to
compare and contrast authors' credibility, facts, argumenta-
tion styles, use of persuasive techniques, and other stylistic
tools. In short, the Opposing Viewpoints Series is an ideal
way to attain the higher-level thinking and reading skills so
essential in a culture of diverse and contradictory opinions.

In addition to providing a tool for critical thinking, Opposing Viewpoints books challenge readers to question their
own strongly held opinions and assumptions. Most people
form their opinions on the basis of upbringing, peer pressure, and personal, cultural, or professional bias. By reading
carefully balanced opposing views, readers must directly
confront new ideas as well as the opinions of those with
whom they disagree. This is not to simplistically argue that

everyone who reads opposing views will—or should—change his or her opinion. Instead, the series enhances readers' understanding of their own views by encouraging confrontation with opposing ideas. Careful examination of others' views can lead to the readers' understanding of the logical inconsistencies in their own opinions, perspective on why they hold an opinion, and the consideration of the possibility that their opinion requires further evaluation.

Evaluating Other Opinions

To ensure that this type of examination occurs, Opposing Viewpoints books present all types of opinions. Prominent spokespeople on different sides of each issue as well as well-known professionals from many disciplines challenge the reader. An additional goal of the series is to provide a forum for other, less known, or even unpopular viewpoints. The opinion of an ordinary person who has had to make the decision to cut off life support from a terminally ill relative, for example, may be just as valuable and provide just as much insight as a medical ethicist's professional opinion. The editors have two additional purposes in including these less known views. One, the editors encourage readers to respect others' opinions—even when not enhanced by professional credibility. It is only by reading or listening to and objectively evaluating others' ideas that one can determine whether they are worthy of consideration. Two, the inclusion of such viewpoints encourages the important critical thinking skill of objectively evaluating an author's credentials and bias. This evaluation will illuminate an author's reasons for taking a particular stance on an issue and will aid in readers' evaluation of the author's ideas.

It is our hope that these books will give readers a deeper understanding of the issues debated and an appreciation of the complexity of even seemingly simple issues when good and honest people disagree. This awareness is particularly important in a democratic society such as ours in which people enter into public debate to determine the common good. Those with whom one disagrees should not be regarded as enemies but rather as people whose views deserve careful examination and may shed light on one's own.

Thomas Jefferson once said that "difference of opinion leads to inquiry, and inquiry to truth." Jefferson, a broadly educated man, argued that "if a nation expects to be ignorant and free . . . it expects what never was and never will be." As individuals and as a nation, it is imperative that we consider the opinions of others and examine them with skill and discernment. The Opposing Viewpoints Series is intended to help readers achieve this goal.

David L. Bender and Bruno Leone,
Founders

Greenhaven Press anthologies primarily consist of previously published material taken from a variety of sources, including periodicals, books, scholarly journals, newspapers, government documents, and position papers from private and public organizations. These original sources are often edited for length and to ensure their accessibility for a young adult audience. The anthology editors also change the original titles of these works in order to clearly present the main thesis of each viewpoint and to explicitly indicate the opinion presented in the viewpoint. These alterations are made in consideration of both the reading and comprehension levels of a young adult audience. Every effort is made to ensure that Greenhaven Press accurately reflects the original intent of the authors included in this anthology.

Introduction

"We must give the public balanced views of the [child abuse] problem and its solution. Yes, we need to hear about the horrible cases of violent and deadly abuse. But we also need to know about the subtler, but equally devastating, cases of neglect and emotional abuse."

—*Donna E. Shalala, former Secretary of Health and Human Services*

In 1995, six-year-old Elisa Izquierdo died at the hands of her mother in New York City. In the sixteen months before Elisa's death, on at least ten occasions, a teacher, a doctor, or a social worker saw physical injuries or "bizarre" behaviors indicative of maltreatment that were either not reported to the state child abuse hotline or were rejected as abuse when a call was made. The wide media attention given Elisa's death resulted in the clarification of New York laws requiring that people such as teachers, doctors, and social workers report suspected incidents of child abuse and prompted an audit of the city's child protective services.

Media coverage of sensational cases such as the death of Elisa can so outrage the public that legislators are forced to take action. At first glance, the public's call to action in response to news of these tragedies would appear to be a good thing for abused children. However, commentators disagree on the impact that media coverage of high profile cases has on the incidence of child abuse. Some believe media attention can benefit abused children while others believe the media further threatens them.

Some analysts assert that media coverage is an important tool for improving public awareness of child abuse. "Because of its major influence on public perception, the media plays a vital role in informing and educating the public," says Evanthe Schurink, program manager of child and family welfare at the Human Sciences Research Council in South Africa. According to Schurink, the more people know about child abuse, the more they are apt to report it: "Members of the public must clearly know what physical, sexual and emotional child abuse is to be able to report child abuse. They must also know what signs to look for to identify the abused child and what to do if they suspect child abuse or if a child discloses abuse." Those who support the attention that the media give to cases of child abuse contend that people are more likely to report child abuse if they are aware of its negative impact.

Others maintain that the media provide an important force for change. According to researchers Chris Goddard and Bernadette J. Saunders, "media coverage is vital if public concern for children is to remain on the political agenda." For example, Goddard and Saunders claim that in Victoria, Australia, the *Herald Sun*'s coverage of the death of two-year-old Daniel Valerio at the hands of his mother's boyfriend, Paul Aiton, led to the introduction of mandatory reporting of suspected incidents of child abuse in Victoria. After the child's death, news coverage revealed that many people had noticed bruising on Daniel, but no action was taken until it was too late. Every day of Aiton's trial the *Herald Sun* published pictures of Daniel's bruised and battered face and a letter demanding the introduction of mandatory reporting. Finally, on March 3, 1993, the front page of the *Herald Sun* read, "Child Abuse Win: Law to Change." Although the result was criticized by some as "legislation by tabloid," those who support media attention argue that the alternative—a public that shows little or no awareness of the child who has been abused or neglected—would be worse.

A number of commentators argue, however, that media coverage of startling cases creates a new set of problems for abused children and their families. Some public satisfaction may come after the offending parent is tried and convicted, the child abuse caseworker is suspended, or child abuse legislation is introduced and quickly passed. But "this approximation of a solution—a solution propelled in good measure by the force of the coverage—sets into motion an entirely new set of problems," journalist Michael Shapiro argues. To protect themselves from the negative media coverage they would receive from having a child die "on their watch," many child abuse caseworkers remove children from their homes without reasonable cause. These children must then be placed in foster homes. Arrangements must be made so that parents who hope to rehabilitate can find jobs, take parenting classes, and submit to drug tests. To meet these needs, the system becomes overburdened and children languish in foster care, where some are abused and even killed, critics contend. Other foster children remain in the system for years, "aging out" at eighteen, often angry and bitter.

Richard Wexler, executive director of the National Coalition for Child Protection Reform, maintains that because the stories written by the media focus on biological parents who kill their children, problems within the foster care system are ignored. Wexler asserts that only thirty-six stories mentioned the death of four-year-old Caprice Reid, who was tied to a chair, denied food and water, and beaten with sticks by her foster parents while over a thousand stories covered the death of Elisa Izquierdo. Moreover, according to the National Committee for the Prevention of Child Abuse, child abuse fatalities are actually relatively rare. The majority of children are removed from their homes for neglect—the failure to provide adequate food, shelter, supervision, or medical care—which is often caused by poverty. Unfortunately, Wexler claims, news stories of the rare cases of biological parents who kill their children guide what journalists report and write about child welfare and, therefore, the public's idea of what policies the government should implement. He argues that this leads to the "creation of policies that have torn thousands of children needlessly from safe and loving—but poor—homes."

Identifying the impact of the media on the development of child abuse policies remains the subject of debate. In *Child Abuse: Opposing Viewpoints* other controversies surrounding the issue of child abuse are debated in the following chapters: What Causes Child Abuse? How Should the Catholic Church Address Child Sexual Abuse? How Should the Legal System Combat Child Sexual Exploitation? How Can Child Abuse Be Reduced? The authors express diverse views about the problem of child abuse and the difficulty of finding effective ways to protect the world's most vulnerable population—its children.

CHAPTER 1

What Causes Child Abuse?

Chapter Preface

While Americans respond with outrage to reports of pedophile priests and the kidnapping, rape, and murder of preadolescent girls, some have begun to question why a nation so opposed to the sexual abuse and exploitation of children continues to tacitly accept the sexualization of children.

Both state and federal legislation demonstrate America's commitment to protect its children from sexual abuse and exploitation. In June 1997, the Supreme Court upheld state laws that allow authorities to indefinitely incarcerate child molesters who pose a continuing threat to children. In California, repeat sex offenders face mandatory chemical castration, and several states have adopted controversial Megan's Laws that allow authorities to notify residents when child molesters have moved into their neighborhood. Although declared unconstitutional, the Child Pornography Prevention Act of 1996 attempted to broaden the scope of federal child-pornography legislation by criminalizing computer-generated simulations of child pornography. These efforts support the view that the nation is dedicated to protecting its children from sexual abuse.

However, that notion was questioned when six-year-old beauty pageant queen JonBenet Ramsey was sexually molested and strangled in the basement of her home in Boulder, Colorado, on December 26, 1996. In *USA Today*, Mark Davidson writes, "The nation must face the disturbing implications of the fact that parents—the very people who should be most outraged by the sexual exploitation of youngsters—have been the principal supporters of hundreds of media-hyped children's 'beauty pageants.'" Following JonBenet's tragic death, the news was flooded with images of her flirtatiously strutting on the pageant stage as a rhinestone cowgirl and a feathered showgirl. Remarking on these images, feminist writer Camille Paglia observes, "the pushy stage mothers of that fast-track beauty-pageant scene seem to have witchily transmuted their daughters into preening baby geishas." These commentators allege that child beauty pageants confirm America's tacit approval of the sexual exploitation of its children.

Some commentators note that the sexualization of children is not limited to beauty pageants but, indeed, seems to permeate American culture. *New York Times* columnist Frank Rich contends that "the flesh-peddling of children in beauty pageants is not a subculture, it's our culture. . . .Today the merchandising of children as sexual commodities is ubiquitous and big business." Those who agree with Rich's assessment point to the full frontal nudity of child-like models in Calvin Klein advertising campaigns. Others condemn retailers who market to preteens who hope to emulate the sexy images of idols such as Britney Spears.

Some analysts point out that Hollywood has long promoted the child as seductress. Both Brooke Shields and Jodie Foster played child prostitutes when they were children. In addition, the 1997 remake of the 1962 film *Lolita* features a forty-year-old man having a sexual relationship with a twelve-year-old girl. Maryam Kubasek of the National Coalition for the Protection of Children and Families remarks, "[the film] panders to the pedophile community in the sense that what they want to believe is that children truly are sexual beings and that to initiate them in the sexual experience is doing them a favor."

Despite these claims, however, no scientific evidence has proven that the sexualized images of children produced by the media encourage pedophilia. Moreover, the media continue to claim First Amendment protection. Since no children were actually harmed in the production of their advertisements or motion pictures, these industries claim, they have not broken any laws. Nevertheless, commentators such as Davidson maintain, "More of America's voices of conscience should demand that the moguls of media stop presenting pedophilia as if it were just another alternative lifestyle."

Controversy continues over whether portraying children as sexual commodities incites pedophiles. The following chapter discusses the sexualization of children and other potential causes of child abuse.

"An 'ecologic' model . . . considers the origin of all forms of child abuse to be a complex interactive process."

Multiple Factors Contribute to Child Abuse

Lesa Bethea

Multiple factors contribute to child abuse, claims Lesa Bethea in the following viewpoint. Although individual factors such as emotional immaturity and substance abuse increase the risk of child abuse, societal factors such as poverty and unaffordable health care also put children at risk, argues Bethea. Child abuse prevention strategies that consider the complex interrelationships among risk factors, Bethea maintains, are more likely to be effective than programs that focus on one cause. Lesa Bethea is a clinical assistant professor of family medicine in the Department of Family and Preventive Medicine at the University of South Carolina School of Medicine, Columbia.

As you read, consider the following questions:

1. Why does the author argue that cause-and-effect models do not accurately predict future cases of child abuse?
2. According to Bethea, what is the most frequently and persistently noted risk factor for child abuse?
3. What three reasons does the author give for the lack of consensus regarding which programs or services should be offered to prevent child abuse?

C hild abuse or maltreatment includes physical abuse, sexual abuse, psychologic abuse, and general, medical and educational neglect. The National Center on Child Abuse and Neglect has established a set of working definitions of the various types of abuse; however, the specific acts that constitute the various forms of abuse are defined under state law and, thus, vary from one jurisdiction to another. For this reason, child abuse is a legal finding, not a diagnosis.

Primary prevention is defined as both the prevention of disease before it occurs and the reduction of its incidence. In the context of child abuse, primary prevention is defined as any intervention designed for the purpose of preventing child abuse before it occurs. This definition encompasses what some authorities have defined as secondary prevention. . . .

This article reviews possible causes of child abuse and current intervention strategies.

The Scope of Child Abuse

Between 1985 and 1993, the number of cases of child abuse in the United States increased by 50 percent. In 1993, three million children in the United States were reported to have been abused. Thirty-five percent of these cases of child abuse were confirmed.

Data from various reporting sources, however, indicate that improved reporting could lead to a significant increase in the number of cases of child abuse substantiated by child protection agencies. The lack of substantiation does not indicate that maltreatment did not occur, only that it could not be substantiated. The fact remains that each year, 160,000 children suffer severe or life-threatening injury and 1,000 to 2,000 children die as a result of abuse. Of these deaths, 80 percent involve children younger than five years of age, and 40 percent involve children younger than one year of age. One out of every 20 homicide victims is a child. Homicide is the fourth leading cause of death in children from one to four years of age and the third leading cause of death in children from five to 14 years of age. Neonaticide (i.e., the murder of a baby during the first 24 hours of life) accounts for 45 percent of children killed during the first year of life.

It is generally accepted that deaths from maltreatment are

underreported and that some deaths classified as the result of accident and sudden infant death syndrome might be reclassified as the result of child abuse if comprehensive investigations were more routinely conducted. Most child abuse takes place in the home and is instituted by persons known to and trusted by the child. Although widely publicized, abuse in day-care and foster-care settings accounts for only a minority of confirmed cases of child abuse. In 1996, only 2 percent of all confirmed cases of child abuse occurred in these settings.

Child abuse is 15 times more likely to occur in families where spousal abuse occurs. Children are three times more likely to be abused by their fathers than by their mothers. No differences have been found in the incidence of child abuse in rural versus urban settings.

Not only do children suffer acutely from the physical and mental cruelty of child abuse, they endure many long-term consequences, including delays in reaching developmental milestones, refusal to attend school and separation anxiety disorders. Other consequences include an increased likelihood of future substance abuse, aggressive behaviors, high-risk health behaviors, criminal activity, somatization [in which psychological needs are expressed in physical symptoms], depressive and affective disorders, personality disorders, post-traumatic stress disorder, panic attacks, schizophrenia and abuse of their own children and spouse. Research has shown that a loving, caring and stimulating environment during the first three years of a child's life is important for proper brain development. This finding implies that children who receive maltreatment in these early years may actually have suboptimal brain development.

The Causes of Child Abuse

Research regarding the causes of child abuse has undergone a paradigm shift. The results of research initiated by the National Research Council's Panel on Research on Child Abuse and Neglect signal the first important step away from simple cause-and-effect models. As was recognized by researchers for the National Research Council's panel, the simple cause-and-effect models have certain limitations, mainly related to their narrow focus on the parents. These models limit themselves by asking only about the isolated set of personal characteristics that might cause parents to abuse or neglect their children. Moreover, these models also fail to account for the occurrence of different forms of abuse in one child. At the same time, these models had very little explanatory power in weighing the value of various risk factors involved in child abuse. As a result, they were not very accurate in predicting future cases of child abuse.

The Path to Child Abuse

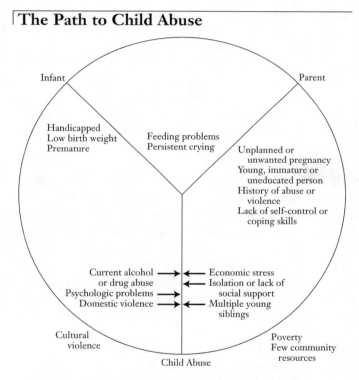

Lesa Bethea, "Primary Prevention of Child Abuse," *American Family Physician*, vol. 59, March 15, 1999.

To replace the old static model, the panel has substituted what it calls an "ecologic" model. This model considers the origin of all forms of child abuse to be a complex interactive process. This ecologic model views child abuse within a system of risk and protective factors interacting across four levels: (1) the individual, (2) the family, (3) the community and (4) the society. However, some factors are more closely linked with some forms of abuse than others.

The Societal Factors

Many would argue that our society does not really value its children. This assertion is highlighted by the fact that one in four children in the United States lives in poverty, and many children do not have any form of health insurance. The presence of high levels of violence in our society is also thought to contribute to child abuse. Deadly violence is more common in the United States than in 17 other developed countries. Seventy-five percent of violence occurring in this country is domestic violence. The United States leads developed countries in homicide rates for females older than 14 years and for children from five to 14 years of age. Other factors that may contribute to high rates of violence include exposure to television violence and reliance on corporal punishment.

Poverty is the most frequently and persistently noted risk factor for child abuse. Physical abuse and neglect are more common among the people who are the poorest. Whether this association is precipitated by the stress of poverty-related conditions or results from greater scrutiny by public agencies, resulting in over-reporting, is debated. Nevertheless, this association is well documented. Other societal factors that have been cited include inaccessible and unaffordable health care, fragmented social services and lack of support from extended families and communities.

The Personal Factors

Parents who were abused as children are more likely than other parents to abuse their own children. However, the retrospective methodology of research in this area has been criticized. Lack of parenting skills, unrealistic expectations about a child's capabilities, ignorance of ways to manage a child's behavior and of normal child development may further contribute to child abuse. It is estimated that 40 percent of confirmed cases of child abuse are related to substance abuse. It is also estimated that 11 percent of pregnant women are substance abusers, and that 300,000 infants are born each year to mothers who abuse crack cocaine. Domestic violence also increases the risk of child abuse.

Other factors that increase the risk of child abuse include emotional immaturity of the parents, which is often highly correlated to actual age (as in the case of teenage parents), poor coping skills, often related to age but also occurring in older parents, poor self-esteem and other psychologic problems experienced by either one or both parents, single parenthood and the many burdens and hardships of parenting that must be borne without the help of a partner, social isolation of the parent or parents from family and friends and the resulting lack of support that their absence implies, any situation involving a handicapped child or one that is born prematurely or at a low birth weight, any situation where a sibling younger than 18 months of age is already present in the home, any situation in which the child is the result of an unwanted pregnancy or a pregnancy that the mother denies, any situation where one sibling has been reported to child protective services for suspected abuse and, finally, the general inherent stress of parenting which, when combined with the pressure of any one or a combination of the factors previously mentioned, may exacerbate any difficult situation.

Examining Primary Prevention Strategies

The U.S. Advisory Board on Child Abuse and Neglect has stated that only a universal system of early intervention, grounded in the creation of caring communities, could provide an effective foundation for confronting the child abuse crisis. It is generally held that successful strategies for preventing child abuse require intervention at all levels of society. However, no consensus has formed regarding which programs or services should be offered to prevent child abuse. In part, this is because research on the prevention of child abuse is limited by the complexity of the problem, the difficulty in measuring and interpreting the outcomes, and the lack of attention to the interaction among variables in determining risk status for subsequent abuse. Although a broad range of programs has been developed and implemented by public and private agencies at many levels, little

23

evidence supports the effectiveness of these programs.

A 1994 retrospective review of 1,526 studies on the primary prevention of child abuse found that only 30 studies were methodologically sound. Of the 11 studies dealing primarily with physical abuse and neglect, only two showed a decrease in child abuse as measured by a reduction in hospital admissions, emergency department visits or reports to child protective services. Although there is a need for better designed research to evaluate the effectiveness of prevention strategies, recommendations for preventive interventions are based on what we currently know about the causes of child abuse.

Social Intervention Strategies

Primary prevention strategies based on risk factors that have a low predictive value are not as likely to be effective as more broadly based social programs. In addition, programs focused on a societal level rather than on the individual level prevent the stigmatization of a group or an individual.

Social strategies for preventing child abuse that are proposed but unproven include increasing the value society places on children, increasing the economic self-sufficiency of families, enhancing communities and their resources, discouraging excessive use of corporal punishment and other forms of violence, making health care more accessible and affordable, expanding and improving coordination of social services, improving treatment for alcohol and drug abuse, improving the identification and treatment of mental health problems, increasing the availability of affordable child care and preventing the births of unwanted children through sex education, family planning, abortion, anonymous delivery and adoption.

Helping the Family

Strategies targeted at the individual can also be considered strategies for helping the family.

Until parents' basic needs are met, they may find it difficult to meet the needs of their children. The first thing parents need is assistance in meeting their basic requirements for food, shelter, clothing, safety and medical care. Only when these needs are met can higher needs be addressed.

The next step should be to identify and treat parents who abuse alcohol or drugs, and identify and counsel parents who suffer from spousal abuse. Identifying and treating parents with psychologic problems is also important. Other issues that need attention include financial concerns, and employment and legal problems. Providing an empathetic ear and being a source of referral for help with these issues may take physicians a long way toward nurturing needy parents.

The next higher level of need includes education about time management and budgeting skills, stress management, coping and parenting skills such as appropriate discipline, knowledge of child development, nutrition and feeding problems, and safety issues.

The Delivery of Services

In the United States, some of the specific methods of delivering services to families include long-term home visitation, short-term home visitation, early and extended postpartum mother/child contact, rooming in, intensive physician contact, drop-in centers, child classroom education, parent training and free access to health care.

Of these methods, only long-term home visitation (up to two years) has been found to be effective in reducing the incidence of child abuse as measured by hospital admissions, emergency department visits and reports to child protective services. Indeed, many organizations are now embracing the concept of home visitation as a method of preventing child abuse by identifying family needs and providing the appropriate services. Results of one study on home visitation showed benefits or improvements in several areas: parents' attitudes toward their children, interactions between parents and children, and reduction in the incidence of child abuse. However, without an infrastructure of support services such as health care, social services and child care, home visitors will be unable to deliver needed services.

"Poverty is by far the most important cause of child maltreatment—and the most important reason families end up in 'the system' whether they have maltreated their children or not."

Poverty Is the Leading Cause of Child Abuse

National Coalition for Child Protection Reform

In the following viewpoint, the National Coalition for Child Protection Reform (NCCPR) maintains that despite claims to the contrary, poverty is the primary cause of child abuse and the reason many children are removed from their homes. According to the NCCPR, state laws define neglect in such a way that it is clear that neglect is caused by poverty. The NCCPR maintains, for example, that parents who must leave their children alone when they go to work because they cannot afford child care can lose their children for "lack of supervision," but the underlying problem is obviously poverty. NCCPR is an organization that opposes foster care and is committed to reforming the child protective system to make it less disruptive to families.

As you read, consider the following questions:
1. According to the authors, what makes a mockery of the claim that children are never removed from their homes because of poverty alone?
2. What examples do the authors provide to explain why the help offered to impoverished families is sometimes a hindrance?

It is an article of faith among "child savers" that "child abuse crosses class lines." They tell us that we are as likely to find maltreatment in rich families as in poor, but the rich can hide from authorities. But like most child saver "truisms," this one is false. Prof. Leroy Pelton, director of the University of Nevada, Las Vegas School of Social Work, calls it "The Myth of Classlessness."

Like the tailors in the fable of "The Emperor's New Clothes," the child savers have invented a whole group of invisible, middle-class child abusers only they are wise enough to see. Of course there are some middle class child abusers. But the evidence is overwhelming that poverty is by far the most important cause of child maltreatment—and the most important reason families end up in "the system" whether they have maltreated their children or not.

Examining the Evidence

The federal government's Third National Incidence Study of Child Abuse and Neglect (NIS-3) compared families with an annual income of under $15,000 to families with an annual income over $30,000. Their findings:

- Abuse is 14 times more common in poor families.
- Neglect is 44 times more common in poor families.

The study emphasized that the findings "cannot be plausibly explained on the basis of the higher visibility of lower income families to community professionals."

Studies in which all the subjects are equally open to public scrutiny (groups made up entirely of welfare recipients, for example) show that those who abuse tend to be the "poorest of the poor."

The Myth of Classlessness doesn't just run counter to research. It runs counter to common sense. It is well-known that child abuse is linked to stress. It is equally well-known that poor families tend to be under more stress than rich families.

The Problem of Neglect

The gap between rich and poor is widest in the area of "neglect"—which makes up by far the largest single category of maltreatment reports. That's because the poor are included in our neglect laws almost by definition.

What is neglect? In Ohio, it's when a child's "condition or environment is such as to warrant the state, in the interests of the child, in assuming his guardianship." In Illinois, it's failure to provide "the proper or necessary support . . . for a child's well-being." In Mississippi, it's when a child is "without proper care, custody, supervision, or support." In South Dakota, it's when a child's "environment is injurious to his welfare."

Such definitions make a mockery of the oft-repeated child-saver claim that "we never remove children because of poverty alone."

Imagine that you are an impoverished single mother with an eight-year-old daughter and a four-year-old son. The four-year-old is ill with a fever and you need to get him medicine. But you have no car, it's very cold, pouring rain, and it will take at least an hour to get to and from the pharmacy. You don't know most of your neighbors and those you know you have good reason not to trust. What do you do?

Go without the medicine? That's "medical neglect." The child savers can take away your children for medical neglect. Bundle up the feverish four-year-old in the only, threadbare coat he's got and take him out in the cold and rain? That's "physical neglect." The child savers can take away your children for physical neglect. Leave the eight-year-old to care for the four-year-old and try desperately to get back home as soon as you can? That's "lack of supervision." The child savers can take away your children for lack of supervision.

And in every one of those cases, the child savers would say, with a straight face, that they didn't take your children "because of poverty alone."

Considering the Cases

Or consider some actual cases from around the country.

- In Orange County, California, an impoverished single mother can't find someone to watch her children while she works at night, tending a ride at a theme park. So she leaves her eight-, six-, and four-year-old children alone in the motel room that is the only housing they can afford. Someone calls child protective services. In-

The Socioeconomic Connection

There is no denying the strong connection between socio-economic status and child maltreatment. For political reasons many have found it important at various points in history to minimize this connection, but today it is widely acknowledged. This does not mean, obviously, that all poor people are destined to abuse or neglect their children. Most do not. And it is of course true that child abuse and neglect occur among all racial groups and on all economic levels. But statistics confirm what the psychological literature and our own experience and common sense suggest: to an overwhelming degree the people who treat their children badly are people who have been treated badly by their own parents and by the larger society. They are people who fall disproportionately into groups that are at the bottom of the socioeconomic ladder.

Elizabeth Bartholet, *Nobody's Children: Abuse and Neglect, Foster Drift, and the Adoption Alternative*, 1999.

---

stead of helping her with babysitting or daycare, they take away the children on the spot.

- In Akron, Ohio, a grandmother raises her 11-year-old granddaughter despite being confined to a wheelchair with a lung disease. Federal budget cuts cause her to lose housekeeping help. The house becomes filthy. Instead of helping with the housekeeping, child protective services takes the granddaughter away and throws her in foster care for a month. The child still talks about how lonely and terrified she was and about the time her foster parent took her picture and put it in a photo album under the heading: "filthy conditions."

- In Los Angeles, the pipes in a grandmother's rented house burst, flooding the basement and making the home a health hazard. Instead of helping the family find another place to live, child protective workers take away the granddaughter and place her in foster care. She dies there, allegedly killed by her foster mother. The child welfare agency that would spend nothing to move the family offers $5,000 for the funeral.

- In Kearney, Missouri, a single mother loses her job as a home health aide, and then loses her rented house. She and her children travel the homeless circuit, moving from friends, to hotels to shelters. The mother wants something better for her children while she gets a job and a place to live so she asks the state child protection agency for help. Instead of providing help with housing and a job, the children are placed in foster care. On the day the mother gets a full-time job, one of her children, a two-year-old girl, dies. An autopsy report calls the death a homicide. The foster mother has been charged. Now the mother has only photos, and a video of the child's funeral. "I asked for help," she said, "and this is what happened," reports Benita V. Williams.

- In Paterson, New Jersey, parents lose their three children to foster care solely because they lack adequate housing. When the children are returned, one of them shows obvious signs of abuse—bruises and new and old burn marks—in foster care. The parents are suing. And so is their first caseworker. He never wanted the children taken away. He'd even found the family a better apartment. But that's not what his superiors wanted. Indeed, the caseworker says that because he insisted on trying to help the family, and refused to alter his reports to make the parents look bad, he was fired. Why were his bosses so anxious to take away the children? There was a rich, suburban couple ready and waiting to adopt them. And according to the lawsuit filed by the caseworker, a supervisor told him that "children should be taken away from poor parents if they can be better off elsewhere," reports Jennifer V. Hughes.

Even when child savers don't remove the children, the "help" they offer impoverished families can be a hindrance. For such families, demanding that they drop everything to go to a counselor's office or attend a parent education class is simply adding one more burden for people who already are overwhelmed.

Step one to ensuring they can provide a safe environment for their children is offering help to ameliorate the worst effects of poverty. Family preservation programs do just that. And that is one reason they succeed where other efforts fail.

"Alcohol, crack cocaine, methamphetamine, heroin and marijuana are fueling [the] population explosion of battered and neglected children."

Substance-Abusing Parents Are More Likely to Abuse Their Children

Joseph A. Califano Jr.

An increase in parental substance abuse is in large part responsible for an increase in child abuse, claims Joseph A. Califano Jr. in the following viewpoint. Califano contends that the homes of abused children are further disrupted when their parents are imprisoned for drug-related felonies. Califano argues that the child welfare system needs to create incentives so that caring and responsible adults will be available to adopt these children, preventing further abuse. Califano, U.S. Secretary of Health, Education, and Welfare from 1977 to 1979, is president of the National Center on Addiction and Substance Abuse at Columbia University in New York City.

As you read, consider the following questions:

1. According to Califano, what percentage of child welfare spending is used to address problems associated with parental substance abuse and addiction?
2. What, in the author's opinion, is the most insidious aspect of parental substance abuse and addiction?
3. Why does Califano believe that the time needed by parents to conquer their substance abuse and addiction is a threat to their children?

Consider the following for a measure of national self-indulgence in the midst of the longest and greatest economic boom in our history. We Americans spend more on cosmetic surgery, hairpieces and make-up for men than we do on child welfare services for battered and neglected children of substance-abusing parents.

A tornado of drug and alcohol abuse and addiction is tearing through the nation's child welfare and family court systems, leaving in its path the wreckage of abused and neglected children, turning social welfare agencies and courts on their heads and uprooting the traditional disposition to keep children with their natural parents.

There is no safe haven for these abused and neglected children of drug- and alcohol-abusing parents. They are the most vulnerable and endangered individuals in America. That is the grim conclusion of an exhaustive two-year analysis by The National Center on Addiction and Substance Abuse at Columbia University.

Parental alcohol and drug abuse and addiction have pushed the nation's system of child welfare to the brink of collapse. From 1986 to 1997, the number of abused and neglected children in America has soared from 1.4 million to some 3 million, a stunning 114.3 percent jump, more than eight times faster than the 13.9 percent increase in the overall children's population. The number of reported abused and neglected children who have been killed has climbed from 798 in 1985 to 1,185 in 1996; the U.S. Advisory Board on Child Abuse and Neglect sets the actual number much higher, at 2,000, a rate of more than five deaths a day.

Fueling the Abuse of Children

Alcohol, crack cocaine, methamphetamine, heroin and marijuana are fueling this population explosion of battered and neglected children. Children whose parents abuse drugs and alcohol are almost three times likelier to be physically or sexually assaulted and more than four times likelier to be neglected than children of parents who are not substance abusers. The parent who abuses drugs and alcohol is often a child who was abused by alcohol- and drug-abusing parents.

Eighty percent of professionals surveyed by CASA said

that substance abuse causes or exacerbates most of the cases of child abuse and neglect they face. Nine of 10 professionals cite alcohol alone or in combination with illegal or prescription drugs as the leading substance of abuse in child abuse and neglect; 45.8 percent cite crack cocaine as the leading illegal substance of abuse; 20.5 percent cite marijuana (which can hardly be considered a benign drug in this situation).

The Cost of Parental Substance Abuse

Parental substance abuse and addiction is the chief culprit in at least 70 percent—and perhaps 90 percent—of all child welfare spending—some $10 billion of the $14 billion that Federal, state and local governments spent simply to maintain child welfare systems in 1998. This $10 billion does not include the costs of health care to abused and neglected children, operating law enforcement and judicial systems consumed with this problem, treating developmental problems, providing special education or lost productivity. Nor does it include the costs attributable to child abuse and neglect that are privately incurred. These costs easily add another $10 billion to the price of child abuse and neglect.

The human costs are incalculable: broken families; children who are malnourished; babies who are neglected, beaten and sometimes killed by alcohol- and crack-addicted parents; eight-year-olds sent out to steal or buy drugs for addicted parents; sick children wallowing in unsanitary conditions; child victims of sodomy, rape and incest; children in such agony and despair that they themselves resort to drugs or alcohol for relief.

Alcohol and drugs have blown away the topsoil of family life and reshaped the landscape of child abuse and neglect in America. Parents addicted to drugs and alcohol are clever at hiding their addiction and are often more concerned about losing their access to drugs and being punished than about losing custody of their children.

For some parents, holding onto their children can provide the motivation to seek treatment. But for many the most insidious aspect of substance abuse and addiction is their power to destroy the natural parental instinct to love and care for their children. Eighty-six percent of professionals surveyed cited lack of motivation as the top barrier to getting such parents into treatment. As Alan Leshner, director of the National Institute on Drug Abuse, has observed, the addicted parent sometimes sees the child as an obstacle to getting drugs.

A Dangerous Shift in Focus

Parental drug and alcohol abuse and addiction have overwhelmed the child welfare system. By 1997 some caseworkers were responsible for 50 cases of child maltreatment at any one time and judges were handling as many as 50 cases a day, giving them less than 10 minutes in an uninterrupted eight-hour day to assess the testimony of parents, social workers, law enforcement officers and others in determining a child's fate.

The Substance Abuse/Child Abuse Link

According to Jeannete L. Johnson and Sis Wenger, "All children wake up in a world that is not of their own making, but children of alcoholics and other drug-addicted parents wake up in a world that doesn't take care of them."

The use and abuse of alcohol and other drugs (AOD) has a profound effect on millions of children and their families and poses a challenge to the capacity of the child welfare system. More than 8 million children in this country live with substance-abusing parents. The impact on child welfare is undeniable: Children whose parents abuse alcohol and other drugs are nearly three times as likely to be abused, and more than four times as likely to be neglected, than are children whose parents are not substance abusers.

Heather Banks and Steve Boehm, *Children's Voice*, September 2001.

Child welfare agencies have been forced to allocate more time to investigations, gathering evidence of neglect and abuse of children by alcohol- and drug-involved parents. This shift in focus has changed the way parents and children see caseworkers and the way these caseworkers view themselves. This shift also threatens to criminalize a process that should be driven by treatment, health care and compassion for both parent and child. The frantic response of many in

Congress and the Clinton Administration is to add felonies to the Federal criminal code and throw more parents in prison—actions likely to do more harm than good for the children of these parents, who need stable and secure homes.

Few caseworkers and judges who make decisions about these children have been tutored in substance abuse and addiction. There are no national estimates of the gap between those parents who need treatment and those who receive it, but Federal Government surveys show that two-thirds of all individuals who need treatment do not get it. There is nothing to suggest that these substance-abusing parents fare any better than the general population.

As the role of substance abuse has increased, the age of the victimized children has gone down. Today most cases of abuse and neglect by substance-abusing parents involve children under five. Alcohol use and binge drinking during pregnancy are up, with at least 636,000 expectant mothers drinking and 137,000 drinking heavily. Some 500,000 babies born each year have been exposed in their mother's womb to cocaine and other illicit drugs (and usually alcohol and tobacco as well). Each year some 20,000 infants are abandoned at birth or kept at hospitals to protect them from substance-abusing parents. The proportion of children whom caseworkers place in foster care at birth jumped 44 percent from the 1983–86 period to the 1990–94 period.

Challenging Parental Rights

Drug and alcohol abuse has thrown into doubt a fundamental tenet of child welfare workers: the commitment to keep the child with his or her natural parents. While terminating parental rights has long been viewed as a failure, alcohol, crack cocaine and other forms of drug abuse have challenged this time honored precept.

There is an irreconcilable clash between the rapidly ticking clock of physical, intellectual, emotional and spiritual development for the abused and neglected child and the slow-motion clock of recovery for the parent addicted to alcohol or drugs. For the cognitive development of young children, weeks are windows of opportunity that can never be reopened. For the parent, recovery from drug or alcohol addiction takes time—and relapse, especially during initial periods of recovery, is common.

Bluntly put, the time that parents need to conquer their substance abuse and addiction can pose a serious threat to their children who may suffer permanent damage during this phase of rapid development. Little children cannot wait; they need safe and stable homes and nurturing adults now in order to set the stage for a healthy and productive life.

Exploring the Solutions

The cruelest dimension of this tragedy for children abused by parents using drugs and alcohol is this: Even when parental rights are terminated in a timely way for such parents who refuse to enter treatment or who fail to recover, in our self-indulgent society there is no assurance of a safe haven for the children. There are not nearly enough adoptive homes. Being in foster care, while far better than being abused, rarely offers the lasting and secure nurturing for full cognitive development, and appropriate foster care is also in short supply. More caring, responsible adults need to step forward to care for the least among us, children of substance-abusing parents.

Child welfare systems and practices need a complete overhaul. Social service providers, from agency directors to frontline child welfare workers, judges, court clerks, masters, lawyers, and health and social service staffs need intensive training in the nature and detection of substance abuse and what to do when they spot it. In all investigations of child abuse and neglect, parents should be screened and assessed for substance abuse. Caseworkers and judges should move rapidly to place children for adoption when parents refuse treatment or fail to respond to it. We need to increase greatly the incentives for foster care and adoption and the number of judges and caseworkers.

Comprehensive treatment that is timely and appropriate, especially for substance-abusing mothers, is essential to prevent further child abuse and neglect. Treatment must be part of a concentrated course that would include mental health services and physical health care; literacy, job and parenting skills training; as well as socialization, employment and drug-free housing. Since most fathers have walked out on their responsibilities, such treatment must be attentive to the fact that most of these parents are women. Where the only hope of reconstituting the natural family for the abused child rests in comprehensive treatment for the parent, it is an inexcusable and vicious Catch-22 situation not to make such treatment available.

Of course, this all costs money. Can we afford to do these things? In the most affluent nation in the history of the world, the answer is a loud and clear yes. Failure to protect these children and provide treatment for their parents who fall prey to drugs and alcohol is more likely than any other shortcoming of survival-of-the-fittest capitalism to bring the harsh judgment of God and history upon us.

In recent years, Pope John Paul II has repeatedly reminded capitalist nations to soften the sharp edges that cut up the least among them. What better way to heed that admonition than to give the needs of these parents and their children first call on the burgeoning Federal budget surplus and the money that the states are picking up from the tobacco settlement.

> *"Children with disabilities were found to be at greater risk of becoming victims of abuse and neglect than children without disabilities."*

Children with Disabilities Are at Greater Risk for Abuse

American Academy of Pediatrics

According to the American Academy of Pediatrics (AAP) in the following viewpoint, children with disabilities are more likely to be neglected and physically and sexually abused than children without disabilities. The authors assert that children with disabilities place higher emotional, physical, economic, and social demands on their families, which increases the risk of abuse by caregivers with limited social or community support. Moreover, the authors maintain, many children with disabilities are considered easy targets because their impaired communication abilities prevent them from disclosing abuse. The AAP supports the health, safety, and well-being of infants, children, adolescents, and young adults.

As you read, consider the following questions:
1. Why is it difficult to evaluate research on the relationship between disabilities and child abuse, according to the academy?
2. What are some of the elements the authors claim increase the risk of abuse for children with disabilities?
3. What, according to the authors, facilitates sexual abuse of disabled children?

The maltreatment of children, including those with disabilities, is a critical public health issue that must be addressed. The Third National Incidence Study of Child Abuse and Neglect showed that the estimated number of abused and neglected children more than doubled between 1986 and 1993. According to a report from the National Child Abuse and Neglect Data System, child protective services (CPS) agencies investigated nearly 2 million reports of alleged maltreatment of an estimated 3 million children in 1995. More than 1 million children were identified as victims of abuse and neglect during that year.

The numbers of children surviving disabling medical conditions as a result of technologic advances and children being recognized and identified as having disabilities are increasing. The rates of child maltreatment have been found to be high with both the child population in general as well as with children who are blind, deaf, chronically ill, developmentally delayed, behaviorally or emotionally disordered, and multiply disabled. Furthermore, child maltreatment may result in the development of disabilities, which in turn can precipitate further abuse. Previous studies have been unable to accurately document the extent or rate of abuse among children with disabilities or determine if disabilities were present before the abuse or were the direct result of maltreatment. Little research on child abuse has focused specifically on children with disabilities.

The Incidence of Abuse Among Children with Disabilities

The Child Abuse and Prevention, Adoption, and Family Services Act of 1988 mandated the study of the incidence of child maltreatment among children with disabilities. This research was funded by the National Center on Child Abuse and Neglect and conducted by the Center for Abused Children With Disabilities at the Boys Town National Research Center. A study by Westat Inc determined the incidence of abuse among children with disabilities and the relationship between child abuse and disabilities. Data were collected from 35 CPS agencies across the country, and results indicated that 14.1% of children whose maltreatment was substantiated by CPS workers had 1 or more disabilities. Disabilities were found to be twice as prevalent among maltreated children in hospitals as among hospital controls, which is consistent with the hypothesis that disabilities increase the risk for maltreatment. However, the data are also consistent with the hypothesis that maltreatment contributes to disabilities.

According to the Boys Town National Research Hospital, children with disabilities were found to be at greater risk of becoming victims of abuse and neglect than children without disabilities. The study showed that children with disabilities are 1.8 times more likely to be neglected, 1.6 times more likely to be physically abused, and 2.2 times more likely to be sexually abused than children without disabilities. The study by Westat Inc determined that, overall, the estimated incidence of maltreatment among children with disabilities was 1.7 times greater than the estimated incidence in children without disabilities. One study found the overall incidence of child maltreatment to be 39% in 150 children with multiple disabilities admitted to a psychiatric hospital. Of those children, 60% had been physically abused, 45% had been neglected, and 36% had been sexually abused.

Examining Research Limitations

A major problem cited by literature is the definition of "disabilities." There is currently no universal definition of what constitutes a disability. The Americans With Disabilities Act defines "disability" as a physical or mental impairment that substantially limits 1 or more of the major life activities of an individual. This definition includes all types of disabilities, including physical disabilities, cognitive or learning disabilities, motor and sensory dysfunctions, mental illness, or any other kind of physical, mental, or emotional impairment. The term "developmental disability" applies to children who have significant developmental delays, congenital abnormalities, or acquired conditions that may result in disability if adequate resources and services are not provided. The term "children with special health care needs" is less limiting than some other terms.

Legal definitions do not always match clinical data. Child development evaluations do not always allow an immediate and precise diagnosis of disability, and some studies rely on evaluations by untrained observers. Therefore, research efforts are hindered by different definitions of terms (eg, disabilities and maltreatment), noncomparable methods, various study sample sizes, and lack of uniform data collection. Furthermore, changes in reporting laws and societal attitudes can occur during a study period.

Getting Rid of Damaged Infants

In 1982, I found this report in the *Archives of Internal Medicine*:

"It is common in the United States to withhold routine surgery and medical care for infants with Down's syndrome for the explicit purpose of hastening death."

Put less delicately, these infants were killed because they were damaged and therefore their "quality of life" did not warrant their growing up. In addition, caring for them would cost a lot and place a heavy emotional burden on their parents.

Nat Hentoff, *Village Voice*, July 1, 1997.

Another problem that has been cited in the literature is the lack of recognition and documentation of disabilities by CPS workers and their lack of training on evaluating children with disabilities. In the study by Westat Inc, analyses were based on CPS workers' opinions rather than data empirically derived from physicians or other professionals trained to diagnose disabilities. B.I. Bonner, S.M. Crow, and L.D. Hensley demonstrated that since 1982, correct and consistent use of the CPS system of collecting information regarding disabilities in maltreated children had decreased, suggesting that disabilities were unlikely to be identified as children enter the CPS system. A survey of 51 state CPS agencies found that in 86% of states, CPS workers used a standardized form to record child maltreatment cases, but in only 59% of those states did the workers record information regarding preexisting disabilities on the form.

The Westat study was limited to intrafamilial cases. Because it is well known that individuals other than family members can commit harm to children, statistics limited to intrafamilial cases would be likely to underestimate the overall incidence of maltreatment among children with disabilities.

The Factors That Increase the Risk

In general, the causes of abuse and neglect of children with disabilities are the same as those for all children; however, several elements may increase the risk of abuse for children with disabilities. Children with chronic illnesses or disabilities often place higher emotional, physical, economic, and social demands on their families. For example, a physical disability that causes difficulty in ambulation can place a child at risk for accidental falls. Therefore, close supervision would be needed. Parents with limited social and community support may be at especially high risk for maltreating children with disabilities, because they may feel more overwhelmed and unable to cope with the care and supervision responsibilities that are required. Lack of respite or breaks in child care responsibilities can contribute to an increased risk of abuse and neglect.

The requirement of special health and educational needs can result in failure of the child to receive needed medications, adequate medical care, and appropriate educational placements, resulting in child neglect. Numerous problems have been cited with the provision of care for foster children with disabilities. Foster parents are sometimes not told about a child's medical and emotional problems and are, therefore, not sufficiently educated or prepared to deal with the specific condition. Other problems for foster children with disabilities include lack of permanent placement, lack of a medical home, lack of financial support, and failure to select appropriate foster parents.

Parents or caregivers may feel increased stress because children with disabilities may not respond to traditional means of reinforcement, and children's behavioral characteristics (ie, aggressiveness, non-compliance, and communication problems, which may appear to be temper tantrums) may become frustrating. A behaviorally challenging child may further increase the likelihood of physical abuse. Parents of children with communication problems may resort to physical discipline because of frustration over what they perceive as intentional failure to respond to verbal guidance. It has been noted, however, that families who report higher stress levels may actually have greater insight into problems associated with caring for a disabled child, whereas parents with a history of neglect of a child may not experience the level of stress that a more involved parent may experience.

Perceptions of Disabled Children

In regard to sexual abuse, infrequent contact of a child with disabilities with others may facilitate molestation, because there is decreased opportunity for the child to develop a trusting relationship with an individual to whom he or she may disclose the abuse. Also, children who have increased dependency on caregivers for their physical needs may be accustomed to having their bodies touched by adults on a regular basis. Children with disabilities who require multiple caregivers or providers may have contact with numerous individuals, thereby increasing the opportunity for abuse. However, an advantage to having a large number of caregivers is that not only may someone detect the injuries or signs of abuse, but also the amount of stress placed on the primary caregiver is decreased.

Children with disabilities often have limited access to critical information pertaining to personal safety and sexual abuse prevention. Parents may object to their child being provided with education on human sexuality. Children with disabilities may also be conditioned to comply with authority, which could result in them failing to recognize abusive behaviors as maltreatment. Children with disabilities are often perceived as easy targets, because their intellectual limitations may prevent them from being able to discern the experience as abuse. Impaired communication abilities may prevent them from disclosing abuse. Because some forms of therapy may be painful (eg, injections or manipulation as part of physical therapy), the child may not be able to differentiate appropriate pain from inappropriate pain.

> *"The natural lines meant to protect children have become dangerously blurred as children, especially girls, have become burdened by the inappropriate transfer of adult sexuality."*

Sexualizing Children May Encourage Child Sexual Abuse

Julie Hudash

Because experts agree that there is a connection between child pornography and pedophilia, argues Julie Hudash in the following viewpoint, parents should not ignore the risk of sexualizing their children. Advertising often treats children as sex objects and encourages young girls to dress and act suggestively, she argues. When society sexualizes children this way, contends Hudash, greater numbers of disturbed individuals will begin to see children as sexual objects. Julie Hudash is a freelance writer who focuses on children's issues.

As you read, consider the following questions:

1. What does Hudash consider a volatile mixture?
2. In the author's opinion, what kinds of shopping experiences should send parents complaining to management and boycotting stores?
3. How does the author compare pedophiles to dry forests during fire season?

Advice on how to protect our children from sexual predators is flying around suburban neighborhoods faster than F-14s over the White House. Parents haunted by the terror of [five-year-old] Samantha Runnion's kidnapping and murder [in Orange County, California, on July 15, 2002] are desperate to ensure the safety of their young ones.

It's never been more clear that monstrous predators exist in all areas of society. No profession or economic class stands immune: clergy, scouting, teaching—there are even allegations that a local judge, with child pornography on his computer, molested a 14-year-old boy.

At the same time, society pressures children into the world of adult sexuality.

The natural lines meant to protect children have become dangerously blurred as children, especially girls, have become burdened by the inappropriate transfer of adult sexuality. This doesn't cause criminal behavior, nor can it serve as an excuse. But it also can't be regarded as benign.

The Child Pornography Connection

The night Samantha's body was found, I listened to four guests on "Larry King Live" discuss the murder. One thing they all agreed upon: the connection between such crimes and child pornography.

Child pornography has exploded on the Internet. This availability encourages the pedophile's sick desire to sexually exploit children. Punishment for creating, distributing or promoting child pornography must be swift, and legislation needs to be in place to lock up these sociopaths.

The terrifying reality of pedophilia, coupled with societal pressures on children to dress and act suggestively, leads to a volatile mixture. This is where parents must take up the fight.

I find myself juggling conflicting motivations. I try to teach our children to be confident and empowered by saying things like "Believe in yourself, and you can be whatever you want to be." Then a voice from deep within says, "But you don't really want to play in the frontyard, do you?"

We must protect these most innocent and vulnerable citizens from a home-bred form of terrorism. Aside from child pornography, children are being dangled as sex objects within the inescapable world of advertising. Recently, Abercrombie & Fitch became embroiled in controversy after it began selling thong underwear for young girls.

Girls in elementary and middle schools feel pressured to keep up with the sexy image of pop star Britney Spears, and retailers are cashing in on the fashion craze.

Luckovich. © 1997 by Mike Luckovich. Reprinted by permission of Creators Syndicate, Inc.

I recently took our preteen daughter shopping for school clothes. It shouldn't be too difficult, I thought, because I had just two requirements. Shirts had to cover the navel, and pants couldn't leave hipbones exposed. It required visits to four stores to find appropriate clothes.

Blurring the Boundaries

A colleague shared a story that illustrates the disappearing boundaries separating childhood, adolescence and adulthood. While shopping at Limited Too, a clothing store popular with pre-teenage girls, she noticed padded bras on sale. She asked the store manager and got this casual response: "Well, you can't imagine how flat some of these girls are!" Exactly! Because they are children, not women!

These kinds of experiences should send parents complaining to management and boycotting the offenders. Where will we draw the line? When our school-age children are wearing stilettos and string bikinis?

Just as kids learn math and reading, they need to learn to understand the visual messages on TV, in music videos, on the computer and in print that bombard them. They must learn critical thinking skills to keep from falling victim to the damaging messages.

I'm a mother of five young children. I don't claim to be an expert in criminology, but I can't disregard the potential impact that the over-sexualizing of our children potentially can have on dangerous pedophiles.

Pedophiles are like dry forests during the peak of fire season—unassuming but potentially dangerous. We can't stop all fires, but we can become aware of the risks and refuse to allow our children to be the spark that ignites disaster.

The pain Samantha's family is enduring is unimaginable. More than flowers, teddy bears and condolence cards, the best way to illustrate that her shortened life served a greater purpose is to fight to protect other children.

Samantha was probably too young to have been affected by the pressure society places on girls. But it's so sadly true that she wasn't too young to fall victim to the undeniable evil in the world.

I can't imagine the terror that Samantha Runnion endured in the last hours of her life. In the words of Marc Klaas, another parent whose daughter was kidnapped and murdered: "No one can turn their backs on this crime anymore."

"*Two of the key contributors to globalization—tourism and the Internet— have provided an unexpected bonus to child abusers, making the opportunity for child abuse more accessible.*"

Globalization Fosters Child Sexual Abuse

Ron O'Grady

Globalization has led to an increase in the child sex trade, claims Ron O'Grady in the following viewpoint. The growth of international tourism as a result of globalization, O'Grady suggests, has enabled pedophiles to move easily from country to country in search of child prostitutes. He maintains, moreover, that the Internet provides pedophiles with access to vulnerable children and, because of its anonymity, shields sexual predators from prosecution. Ron O'Grady, of New Zealand, is the founder of the international organization End Child Prostitution, Child Pornography, and Trafficking (ECPAT), and author of *The Rape of the Innocent*.

As you read, consider the following questions:

1. What prevailing view does the author suggest keeps the tourism industry from participating in efforts to combat child sex tourism?
2. What three features of the Internet have special significance for pedophiles?
3. According to O'Grady, what happens to child sex abusers under laws of extraterritoriality?

Ron O'Grady, "Eradicating Pedophilia: Toward the Humanization of Society," *Journal of International Affairs*, vol. 55, Fall 2001, pp. 123–30. Copyright © 2001 by *Journal of International Affairs*. Reproduced by permission.

While child sex abuse is now out of the closet and in the public arena, there is scattered evidence to suggest that the number of children caught in prostitution, pornography or trafficking is increasing. Two of the key contributors to globalization—tourism and the Internet—have provided an unexpected bonus to child abusers, making the opportunity for child abuse more accessible. One could draw a partial causal relationship between the rapid expansion of globalization and the growth of child sex trade.

The Growth of Sex Tourism

Tourism has become the world's largest industry and its long arms reach out into ever more obscure parts of the planet. With a constant increase of at least four to five percent in tourism numbers every year, the exponential growth develops a world of transients. Conservative estimates of the World Tourism Organization indicate that by the year 2020, tourism movements will reach 1.6 billion persons per annum.

The study of tourism first pointed out the existence of child prostitution in the developing world. The phenomena known as "sex tourism" grew rapidly in Asia following the Vietnam War, as Japanese and American male tourists joined group tours, whose function was primarily to have sexual adventures in countries such as the Philippines and Thailand.

When social workers began to ask questions, it soon became apparent that within this new form of tourism there was a sub-culture of pedophiles developing their own form of "sex tourism." Lax law enforcement and easy access to desperate families made some countries the pedophiles' favorite destinations.

While such visible tour groups no longer occur, organized networks of tourist pedophiles still operate. They share information on the best destinations, and as some countries clamp down on child sex tourists, they begin to frequent other countries. The increased number of foreigners arrested and convicted for child abuse in countries such as Sri Lanka, Thailand and the Dominican Republic suggests that child sex tourism remains a popular activity for pedophiles.

The tourism industry has been slow to recognize the serious nature of child sex tourism. When the issue came to prominence in 1989, some tourism leaders were quick to distance themselves from any responsibility. The head of a major European airline firm publicly stated that airlines are like people who sell hammocks. He argued that if a man buys a hammock and then uses the string to hang himself, the hammock manufacturer cannot be blamed for his death.

A similar view continues to prevail among many sections of the tourism industry. The belief is that the tourism emphasis must always be uncompromisingly positive and that matters such as child sex tourism need to be addressed by governments and social service groups, but not by the industry itself. Tourism is there, they will argue, to provide services and meet the dreams of the people. If some people abuse that opportunity, the tourism industry cannot be blamed.

Since 1997, tourism leaders have begun to recognize that they have to assume some corporate responsibility. Tourism is not to blame for child sex abuse, but tourism is the context in which it occurs and therefore must be addressed. The World Tourism Organization has established a task force to monitor the development of child sex tourism and seek ways to combat it. Related groups including the Universal Federation of Travel Agents' Associations and the airline group IATA have also made strong statements. In Europe, major travel organizations in five countries are experimenting with a code of conduct that is specifically designed to provide a mechanism for educating the tourism industry.

These are all positive developments. In places where child prostitution takes place, the people working in the tourism industry would be the first to recognize its presence. In the past, tour guides, hotel keepers, airline staff and many other tourism-related workers have persistently turned a blind eye to the actions of their customers. But if workers in the tourism industry are made aware of the damage being done to their own culture and their own children by the actions of some tourists, they would become more active in reporting such cases to the authorities.

An example of what is possible occurred on an Air India flight in 1992. The flight attendant was made aware that a young girl passenger was being abducted from her home in Hyderabad by an older Arabian man, who regularly took children from India to his home country to become sex slaves. So, she radioed ahead to Delhi. When the plane stopped in transit, the police boarded the aircraft and took the child away from the procurer. Ironically, the flight attendant who prevented this crime was chastised and suspended from her work for becoming involved in something that was outside her professional responsibility.

Adding to the Problem

There have been some side effects of the tourism boom that have encouraged child trafficking. The tourism industry continues to pressure governments to reduce border controls to ease the flow of tourists. With few or no border checks, the movement of children from one country to another becomes a simple matter.

Sex with Children Is a Crime

It has long been illegal for adults to have sex with children in the U.S. But under a new federal law it is now illegal for Americans to travel overseas to have sex with children under 18. Many countries are enacting tough new laws to stop the abuse, exploitation and murder of young children. Penalities for sexual abuse of children are being increased. The age of consent has been raised in some countries. Laws against transporting girls and women for the sex industry are being made tougher. Countries are putting more emphasis on enforcement of these laws.

The U.S. is getting tough too. Anyone found guilty of having gone abroad for sex with a girl or boy—whether a prostitute or not—can be imprisoned for up to 10 years, fined or both. Bringing or sending child pornography into the U.S. can lead to arrest. Making child pornography overseas and planning to bring it, send it, distribute it, or have someone else distribute it in the U.S. can lead to arrest.

End Child Prostitution, Child Pornography, and Trafficking of Children for Sexual Purposes (ECPAT-USA), *What You Should Know About Sex Tourism.*

Europe is struggling to control the trade in women and children. In 2001, more than 10,000 Moldovan women, some as young as 12 years of age, are believed to have been kidnapped or coaxed to the West by the promise of jobs, only to be forced into prostitution. Non-governmental organizations estimate that between 1 million and 2 million women are trafficked annually. In Europe, about 50,000 women, many of whom are minors, are introduced to the sex slave market each year.

Since the fall of the Communist bloc in Eastern Europe, organized crime in that region has found the abduction and trafficking of children to be a lucrative market. War, poverty and social unrest have provided a milieu in which children can easily be separated from parents and speedily moved to another country. Once there, they are totally dependent on their new masters. As illegal aliens they are without rights, possess no identification and have no language or means of communication. It is a form of total slavery from which there appears to be no escape.

A second contributor to globalization has become important for any consideration of the growth of child sex abuse—the Internet. There are three features of the net which have special significance for pedophiles:

The Anonymity of the Internet

1. The anonymity of the net means that pedophiles can speak to each other in relative privacy. When the message is encrypted, the chance of discovery diminishes. The development of extensive international pedophile networks has proved to be a giant validating mechanism for pedophiles. Aware of the fact that most of society finds their actions repugnant, they can get solace from friendship with fellow believers.

   Some have even convinced themselves that they are the vanguard for the new world. They argue that just as homosexuality was once secretive and unacceptable behavior that is now out of the closet, so too child sex will one day become accepted as normal and healthy. Such arguments completely disregard the difference between the consensual nature of homosexual acts between consenting adults and against the one-sided coercion and manipulation involved in pedophilic acts.

   In the anonymity of the Internet, pedophiles gain information that is important to them in their attempts to seduce children. They share experiences, compare laws, discuss techniques for entrapment and talk of their travels to the latest pedophile paradise.

Sharing Collections of Child Pornography

2. The ability to share actual images of child sex abuse either through pornographic photographs or video clips on the Internet gives them a quick and easy way to develop huge collections of child pornography by exchanging images within a network. As mentioned earlier, one of the distinctive traits of pedophiles is their desire to collect and document their own exploits.

A new and disturbing development is the use of videos attached to computers that enables pedophiles linked to an international network to watch the sexual abuse of children in real-time and to interact with the abuser. Police are aware of a number of such groups and two international rings have been broken through international police cooperation. The Orchid Club based in the United States was uncovered in 1998 and an even more sophisticated group, the Wonderland Club, was broken in 2001. The latter club had members in several countries and was strictly monitored with complicated passwords and initiation requirements. Only an accident on the part of one of the members in 1996 enabled a customs probe to learn of the club. It took another four years to uncover the full extent of the Club's activities. More than 100 people in 21 countries were arrested on 2 September 2000, and police took over a cache of more than 750,000 images of child pornography of children as young as 18 months.

The quantum of child pornography on the net increases monthly. A single photo placed on the web can multiply several thousand times in 24 hours. It is important to realize that behind each of these photos is a real child somewhere who has to go through life knowing that the trauma of their abuse is on the net in perpetuity. It becomes a huge burden for young people to carry and helps explain the number of abused children that commit suicide in later life.

Hunting for Victims

3. Child sex abusers are predatory and the net provides them with a new facility for their actions. Pedophiles no longer have to sit in automobiles in front of school gates watching for children to abuse. Now they can hunt for them on Internet chat rooms. It is deceptively simple. The pedophile has a fixation on finding a victim of a particular age and sex. He has become an expert on the tastes of children that age. He knows what music they listen to, what games they play and the vocabulary they use in their school conversations. By pretending to be one of them, the pedophile can cultivate a friendship. At some point, conversations turn toward sexual matters. Finally, as recorded in a number of documented cases, the pedophile arranges to meet the child in a quiet place, where the abuse will take place. Parents need to be made aware of this possibility and provide their children with rules about safety on the net.

A Need for International Cooperation

In a changing world it is no longer possible to consider the commercial sexual abuse of children in the context of the laws of a single country. The development of the Internet is, in itself, a major reason why efforts must be made to harmonize international laws to protect children. The Internet knows no boundaries and no country can protect itself from the deluge of information pouring in from the 214 countries now connected to it. . . .

The Internet continues to play a major role in the lives of child sex abusers and is proving very difficult to combat. The Internet is an anarchic force that defies control. With more than 7.3 million new documents being posted on the net every day, it has become impossible for any law enforcement agency to keep watch on the content that is entering their country from every other country in the world. Experiments with blocking software and virus attacks have had only limited success.

International co-operation will have to be the way of the future. In areas of law enforcement, the international policing agency, Interpol, has established an experts group that meets twice a year to deal with crimes against minors. Drawing on police resources in many countries, they have developed new strategies for sharing information and countering the crime of child sex abuse and trafficking. In addition to expanding their cooperative work, the strategy for the future includes the development of better intelligence through hotlines, creation of rating and filtering tools for the Internet, and more media awareness and public education.

Creating Laws for a Global Society

Changing laws to make them more effective in the global society has been an important part of the lobby effort against the sexual trade of children. When the significance of sex tourism became apparent ten years ago, a major obstacle was the manner in which the laws against child abuse focused solely on the national law. Dozens of instances were noted of Europeans or Americans abusing children in Asia, paying a small sum to the police and going home with no criminal record against their name. The scandal of such actions led to an organized lobbying of governments by End Child Prostitution, Child Pornography and Trafficking (ECPAT) to introduce laws of extraterritoriality. Under such laws, child sex abusers, who commit a crime against children in another country, can be convicted and punished for their crime in their home country.

At first, most governments argued that such an action was unconstitutional. But when Germany became the first country to introduce a law of extraterritoriality in September 1993, the flood-gates opened. Soon every country in Europe, North America, Australia and several other places had introduced a similar law. Since then, this law has regularly and effectively been implemented, particularly in Western Europe and Australia.

Despite considerable international activity, there is still a long way to go in understanding the seriousness of the crime of child sex abuse and the way it continues to affect our societies. In many countries, law enforcement officers make child abuse a low priority. The judiciary often reinforces this attitude by giving nominal sentences to child abusers or those producing child pornography. In an effort to redress this situation, a few countries have established a national register of convicted pedophiles. This register can be consulted under strict guidelines by schools and organizations wanting to appoint staff that will be in close working contact with children. . . .

Society will always be judged by the way it treats its most vulnerable members. When it ignores the abuse of its own children, it creates social problems that will last long into the future and cause tensions that cannot be resolved. Perhaps the rate of guilt-ridden suicide will increase or the unproven cycle of victim turning abuser will repeat itself. In some instances, the concept of family will break down. The development of children must be our primary concern. To prevent further destruction, society must provide care, protection and guidance to its own children. This has always been humankind's greatest challenge and will continue to remain so. As we enter the 21st century our best efforts must be directed toward the humanization of society through the nurture of our children.

Periodical Bibliography

The following articles have been selected to supplement the diverse views presented in this chapter.

John A. Barnes	"The Boyfriend Problem," *Weekly Standard*, December 14, 1998.
Bridgett A. Besinger et al.	"Caregiver Substance Abuse Among Maltreated Children Placed in Out-of-Home Care," *Child Welfare*, March/April 1999.
Tucker Carlson	"Horror in the Court: How a Mother Who Murders One Child Can Keep Another," *Weekly Standard*, January 26, 1998.
Jennifer Clarke et al.	"Victims as Victimizers," *Archives of Internal Medicine*, September 13, 1999.
Joseph Collision	"What the Pope Called the 'Culture of Death' Is Actually a Syndicate of Death," *New Oxford Review*, January 1998.
Perle Slavik Cowen	"Child Neglect: Injuries of Omission," *Pediatric Nursing*, July/August 1999.
Mark Davidson	"Is the Media to Blame for Child Sex Victims?" *USA Today Magazine*, September 1997.
John J. Dilulio Jr.	"Twilight of Authority," *Weekly Standard*, May 3, 1999.
Agustin Gurza	"Concocting a Cultural Excuse for Child Abuse," *Los Angeles Times*, February 29, 2000.
Nat Hentoff	"Getting Rid of Damaged Infants," *Village Voice*, July 1, 1997.
Philip Jenkins	"Mommy's Little Monster: Does the Family Breed Serial Killers?" *Chronicles*, May 1999.
Patrick T. Murphy	"A Trap of Welfare and Child Abuse," *New York Times*, August 11, 2000.
Mary D. Overpeck et al.	"Risk Factors for Infant Homicide in the United States," *New England Journal of Medicine*, October 22, 1998.
Robert Scheer	"The Dark Side of the New World Order: The Increased Selling of Young Women into Sex Slavery Is the Latest Global Commodity," *Los Angeles Times*, January 13, 1998.
Viera Scheibner	"Shaken Baby Syndrome: The Vaccination Link," *Nexus*, August/September 1998.

CHAPTER 2

How Should the Catholic Church Address Child Sexual Abuse?

Chapter Preface

In 1984, the first year of his assignment to the Boston diocese, Cardinal Bernard Law approved the transfer of Father John J. Geoghan to St. Julia's parish in Weston, Massachusetts, despite substantial evidence that Geoghan had sexually abused children during previous assignments. Geoghan had been treated several times for molesting boys and had been removed from at least two parishes for sexually abusing children.

In 1989 Geoghan was again forced to take sick leave after complaints that he was sexually abusing children. Once again he was treated and returned to the parish where he continued to abuse children until 1993, when he was finally removed from parish duty. Since the mid-1990s, more than 130 people have come forward with allegations that the former priest fondled or raped them in incidences spanning three decades. However, not until 1998 did the church actually remove Geoghan from the priesthood. Ultimately, in February 2002, Geoghan was sentenced to ten years in prison for sexually abusing a ten-year-old boy.

Allegations of a cover-up by Cardinal Law and the Catholic Church did not become a national controversy, however, until January 6, 2002, when *The Boston Globe* ran the following headline on its front page—"Church Allowed Abuse by Priest for Years." In the months that followed, the national media reported a stream of cases that linked Catholic priests to child sexual abuse. By April 2002 at least 177 priests had been removed from their duties, and one priest, Father Don Rooney, committed suicide after being accused of abusing a young female parishioner twenty-two years earlier. News reports also revealed that by the mid-1990s, the church faced more than two hundred lawsuits defending allegations of sexual abuse that cost the church $400 million in settlements, legal fees, and medical expenses.

What surprised most people was not that some priests sexually abused children, but that the church knew of patterns of sexual abuse of children by some of its priests yet continued to allow these men access to children. Catholic clergy and laity alike began to question the way the church handled cases of child sexual abuse. At first, Catholic officials tried to depict the problem as one blown out of proportion by the media. According to Mark Chopko, general counsel of the U.S. Conference of Catholic Bishops, "There is no cover-up. People are confusing protecting the privacy of some individuals involved with the view that there's been persistent criminal conduct by the leadership of the church."

However, outraged clergy and parishioners disagreed. According to Father Gary Hayes, president of the group Linkup: Survivors of Clergy Abuse and himself a victim of abuse by two priests while a teenager, "while individual bishops and dioceses have responded well to this crisis, the church as a whole has responded with arrogance, defiance, ignorance, and indifference . . . the real problem is that we have a hierarchy more interested in protecting its image than the innocence of its children."

In April 2002, after four months on the defensive, Catholic leaders from the United States gathered at the Vatican to come up with a strategy to deal with the crisis. The meetings ended with an apology for allowing the scandal to happen and a proposal to dismiss any priest guilty of "serial" sexual abuse of minors. However, this communiqué called for a separate process to deal with those priests guilty of serial, predatory sexual abuse of minors and those considered only a threat. Moreover, it was not clear whether those priests accused of past abuse would be defrocked.

People continue to debate whether the Catholic Church has done enough to protect children from predatory priests. The following chapter offers several perspectives on how the Catholic Church should address the problem of child sexual abuse by its clergy.

1

| *"Time will show that the bishops' actions were both prudent and in the best interests of all in society, especially our children."*

The Catholic Church's Response to Child Sexual Abuse Is Adequate

Stephen J. Rossetti

According to Stephen J. Rossetti in the following viewpoint, the Catholic Church has responded in the best interests of the children when handling cases of child sexual abuse. For example, Rossetti claims that the church has reassigned priests accused of child sexual abuse to supervised positions. Unfortunately, Rossetti argues, an uninformed public has pressured the church to dismiss such priests, an action that would release child abusers into society unsupervised, which could result in an increase in cases of child sexual abuse. Rossetti is a psychologist and president of St. Luke Institute, a private Catholic psychiatric hospital serving clergy. He is also a consultant to the U.S. Conference of Catholic Bishops' ad hoc committee on child sexual abuse.

As you read, consider the following questions:

1. Why does Rossetti believe it is an error to apply the same remedy to all adults who sexually abuse minors?
2. What does the author believe should shock people about the conclusions of his survey?
3. According to the author, what are two problems with the suggestion that bishops should report all allegations of child sexual abuse?

Stephen J. Rossetti, "The Catholic Church and Child Sexual Abuse: Distortions, Complexities, and Resolutions," *America*, vol. 186, April 22, 2002, pp. 8–15. Copyright © 2002 by America Press, Inc., 106 West 56th St., New York, NY 10019. www.americamagazine.org. Reproduced by permission.

W hen complex situations are given simplistic understandings and simplistic solutions, people will in-
evitably be hurt. The phenomenon of child sexual abuse, in
the priesthood and in society at large, is a complex issue that
does not admit of simple understandings or simple solutions.
It is important that we examine the issue in greater depth;
otherwise the church and society will not only repeat past
mistakes but also make new mistakes in response. Most important, without a more informed understanding and a more
reasoned response, children will be no safer and may, inadvertently, be placed at even greater risk.

Examining Misconceptions

I would like to discuss five major oversimplifications and distortions regarding child sexual abuse that have been publicly
raised during April 2002.

1. All child molesters are pedophiles and all pedophiles
are incurable. They are dangerous men who abuse scores of
minors. There is no hope for them.

As with all distortions, there is some truth to these statements. There are child molesters who are pedophiles, that is,
they are sexually attracted to pre-pubescent minors, and
some molest scores of minors. These high-profile, notorious
abusers, who capture public attention, are usually resistant
to psychological treatment. One does not speak of trying to
change or "cure" their sexual attraction to minors. While
some pedophiles can be helped to control their sexual de-
sires, many cannot. Since these persons pose an ongoing
threat to society, after serving an appropriate prison term,
they ought to live in a kind of lifelong parole setting with absolutely no unsupervised contact with minors.

Fortunately, real pedophiles are the exception among
adults who sexually abuse minors. Most abusers are not pedophiles. Most abuse post-pubescent minors and, all things
being equal, are much more amenable to treatment. While
both pedophiles and those who molest post-pubescent minors have committed a heinous crime, it would be an error
to apply exactly the same remedy to them all. With treatment and supervision, many adults who molest adolescents
can go on to live productive lives. But prudence would still

dictate that these adults should be supervised whenever interacting with adolescents. . . .

Questioning a Celibate Priesthood

2. Priests are more likely to be child molesters than others because they are celibate. Celibacy distorts one's sexuality, and a celibate priesthood attracts a larger proportion of men with sexual problems.

The first half of this simplification has been largely discredited in recent media stories. Researchers and clinicians have generally accepted the fact that celibacy does not cause child sexual abuse. In fact, the sexual difficulties and inner psychological problems that give rise to child sexual abuse are largely in place long before a person enters into the formation process for a celibate priesthood. In addition, most adults who sexually molest minors are, or will be, married.

The second half of the statement, "a celibate priesthood attracts a larger proportion of men with sexual problems," is currently being debated. Some have said that we seem to have so many child molesters in the priesthood because celibacy attracts people with sexual problems. Is that true?

It is a complex problem that demands a complex answer. Some people with sexual problems seek out a celibate lifestyle in an unconscious attempt to escape their own sexuality. I know this for a fact because I have counseled some who admit the same. Nonetheless, it is dangerous to summarize from the particular to the general. . . .

Evaluating Basic Assumptions

This brings to light the basic assumption that underlies these distortions—namely, that priests are more likely to be child abusers than others in society. Is that true? The short answer is: we do not know. There are simply no prevalence rates of perpetration of child sexual abuse either in society at large or in the priesthood. The reason for the lack of data is inherent in the crime. It is very difficult to gather a sample of adult males and ask them if they have ever sexually abused a minor. Even if they told the truth, gathering such data would present thorny ethical and legal considerations. . . .

While one case is one too many, especially when perpetrated by a man with a sacred trust—a Catholic priest—the suggestion that priests are more likely to be child abusers than other males has yet to be established. In fact, the early statistics challenge that assumption and actually imply that the number of priests who molest could be lower. It would be reasonable to believe that the number of adult males who molest minors in society is at least as large. One need only speak with the dedicated and overworked social workers who staff our child protective services around the country to know that the percentage of adult males who molest minors is not insignificant. I conducted a survey of 1,810 adults in the United States and Canada and found that over 19 percent of them had been the victims of sexual molestation by an adult before the age of 18. This suggests that there are many perpetrators of child sexual abuse in our society. While we are shocked, and rightly so, that there would be 60 priests in the Archdiocese of Boston who have molested minors, we should be equally shocked at just how common child sexual abuse is throughout our society.

Interpreting the Link to Homosexuality

3. We have so many child abusers in the priesthood because a celibate priesthood attracts homosexuals.

No mainstream researcher would suggest that there is any link between homosexuality and true pedophilia, that is, sexual attraction of an adult to prepubescent minors. In addition, most adults in society who sexually molest minors are not homosexually oriented.

The rejoinder to this is the fact that most victims of priests are young males. But this, too, is easily open to misinterpretation. Most priests who molest minors were themselves molested as minors; their sexual abuse of minors is for many of them a kind of re-enactment of their own abuse and may have little to do with their sexual orientation. I have known some heterosexually oriented males who molested young males.

Nonetheless, a significant number of priests who sexually molest minors are involved with post-pubescent adolescent males, about 14 to 17 years of age. It appears to be true that many in this sub-population of priest child-molesters are homosexually oriented. But theirs is a particular kind of homosexuality, which one might call "regressed" or "stunted." These homosexual men are emotionally stuck in adolescence themselves, and so are at risk for being sexually active with teenage males. The issue is therefore not so much homosexuality but rather their stunted emotional development.

The problem is not that the church ordains homosexuals. Rather, it is that the church has ordained regressed or stunted homosexuals. The solution, then, is not to ban all homosexuals from ordained ministry, but rather to screen out regressed homosexuals before ordination. Preparation for ordination should directly assess the seminarian's ability and commitment to live a chaste, celibate life.

We are in a dangerous period that is intensely emotional. Everyone, inside and outside the church, wants to find simplistic solutions. "Getting rid of homosexuals" from the priesthood will not be as successful as some predict in ridding the church of child abusers and in the end may cause even more human damage.

The Reporting Requirement

4. The U.S. bishops continue to be secretive about child sex abuse cases and fail to follow the law and report these cases to legal authorities. They cannot be trusted.

Much of the real energy behind the current furor is anger directed at the Catholic bishops. People feel betrayed. But since 1992 I have witnessed bishops tackling scores of cases with great care and solicitude for victims and perpetrators. Yet they are currently being depicted as being grossly negligent. How can we understand this apparent contradiction?

It is true that in a minority of cases, victims have been asked to sign "gag orders." The diocese agrees to settle a civil suit; it pays out a certain sum of money, and it stipulates that the victim will not publicly reveal what happened. In retrospect, this can be recognized as a mistake. While one can understand a bishop's desire not to "scandalize" people and to protect the church's image, such actions promote distrust and allegations of secrecy.

Nevertheless, it is not true that bishops are circumventing the reporting requirements about child sexual abuse. Again, the reality is much more complicated. In most states, child-abuse reporting laws require that suspected incidents be reported only if the victim who comes forward is still a minor. I called one state's child protective services and asked if they would investigate a report if the victim was no longer a minor. The answer was no.

What Percentage of Priests Are Abusers?

- Philip Jenkins is a professor of history and religious studies at Penn State University, and has written a book on the topic. He estimates that 2% of priests sexually abuse youth and children.

- Richard Sipe is a psychotherapist and former priest, who has studied celibacy and sexuality in the priesthood for four decades. He has authored three books on the topic. By extrapolating from his 25 years of interviews of 1,500 priests and others, he estimates that 6% of priests abuse. Of these, 4% abuse teens, aged 13 to 17; 2% abuse pre-pubertal children.

- Sylvia M. Demarest, a lawyer from Texas, has been tracking accusations against priests since the mid-1990s. By 1996, she had identified 1,100 priests who had been accused of molesting children. She predicts that when she updates the list, the total will exceed 1,500 names. This represents about 2.5% of the approximately 60,000 men who have been active priests in the U.S. since 1984. It is important to realize that these are accused priests; the allegations have not been evaluated in a trial. Also, there is no way to judge what proportion of abusive priests are on her list. It may include 40% or fewer; she may have found 90% or more.

- Columnist Ann Coulter claimed, without citing references, that there are only 55 *"exposed abusers"* in a population of 45,000 priests. This is an abuse rate of 0.12%.

ReligiousTolerance.org, May 17, 2002.

One might then suggest that the bishop report the allegation of abuse to the criminal authorities. There are two problems with this. First of all, the law does not require the bishop to report the allegation if the victim is no longer a minor and the bishop has a concurrent obligation to maintain pastoral confidentiality with those who confide in him, just as a secular counselor would. If the law does not give him "permission" to break confidentiality and report the abuse, then he is obligated to protect confidentiality. Second, even if he did report the allegation of abuse to the criminal authorities, the statute of limitations may well have expired, and there is little hope that the justice system would be of any assistance. Unfortunately, only a minority of cases of child sexual abuse are successfully adjudicated criminally. . . .

The bishops are being excoriated for not reporting cases of abuse. But the laws do not require it in most situations that the church faces. The bishops also have a pastoral obligation to maintain confidentiality. What many dioceses are doing is counseling the victims that they themselves are free to report the incident to civil authorities. In fact, the church should encourage victims to report such an incident. But one can clearly argue that unless the law requires the church to break confidentiality—which the law usually does not do—it is up to the victim to report. . . .

The Problem of Re-Offenders

5. The safest thing for children is to defrock any priest who is guilty of child sexual abuse. The church has been grossly negligent by continuing to shuffle such priests from parish to parish, where they re-offend.

It is true that the Archdiocese of Boston made a grievous error in reassigning John Geoghan to a parish after he became known as a child molester. There was no excuse for such an action. Any priest who sexually molests a minor should never be returned to parish ministry or any ministry involving minors. But I would say clearly that there have been very few cases of such actions since 1992. Even in Boston, almost all the priests with substantial allegations of child sexual abuse were either retired early, dismissed from ministry or placed in assignments not involving minors. Even in Boston, the case of John Geoghan is an exception, but it is being portrayed as if it were normal in the church.

This raises a more difficult question: should any priest who has a past history of molesting a minor remain in the priesthood? Clearly, the public is saying no. And I think public pressure will have its way. Around the country, priests with a substantial allegation of child molestation are being dismissed from any form of ministry. The damage to the church's credibility is so large, and the legal and financial fallout is so great, that many of our leaders feel forced to expel them all. This is certainly the safest action for the church.

The Risk of an Absolute Policy

But is this the safest course of action for children? When priests are dismissed from ministry, they go out into society unsupervised and perhaps even untreated. Then they are free to do as they please. If they have been convicted of a sexual crime against minors, they may have to be registered in compliance with various state or local laws. But, as noted previously, there are few criminal convictions against child sex abusers. Either the statute of limitations has run out, or the victim does not want a criminal trial, or there is simply insufficient evidence. Whatever the reason, when the church "defrocks" these priests, they are no longer supervised. One might recall the case of James Porter, who was expelled from the Diocese of Fall River in Massachusetts and returned to life as a layman. He married and was eventually convicted of molesting his children's baby sitter.

The question of what to do with child molesters is complex. Some bishops have been sending priests accused of child sexual abuse for intensive psychotherapeutic treatment and then, depending upon the man's response to treatment, taking the ones who present the least risk and returning them to a limited, supervised ministry that did not involve direct contact with minors. Of the scores of such cases, very, very few have re-offended. The public has been outraged that these men were still in ministry at all. But I believe that time will show that the bishops' actions were both prudent and in the best interests of all in society, especially our children. If all these priests had been summarily dismissed from the priesthood, it is very probable that more children would have been abused. Putting a priest through treatment and leaving him in a limited ministry, such as that of chaplain to a convent or nursing home, is not without some risk. But there is more risk in releasing him into society.

In general, the bishops of the United States have done well

in dealing with most cases of child sexual abuse by priests since 1992. There have been exceptions, and mistakes have been made. But there will always be mistakes made with such complex and difficult cases. On the surface, the matter seems easy. The public says, "The priest is charged with sexual abuse, so throw him out of the priesthood." But if the civil and criminal authorities will not prosecute the case—and in most cases they will not—who decides if the accused is guilty? Unfortunately and unfairly, this falls to the bishops. They have tried to do what is right and best for everyone. But public pressure is forcing them to dismiss them all. The bishops are acquiescing, and now these men become society's problem, not just the church's. I hope that society handles these cases well.

*"The credibility of the [church] hierarchy
will not be restored by mere words—more
decrees, more public apologies, more
promises of 'no more abuse.'"*

The Catholic Church's Response to Child Sexual Abuse Is Inadequate

Thomas P. Doyle

Rather than take action to address the problem, the hierarchy of the Catholic Church shifts the blame and makes excuses for its inadequate reaction to cases of child sexual abuse by its clergy, writes Thomas P. Doyle in the following viewpoint. To solve the problem, he maintains, the hierarchy must change its attitude from protecting the image of the Catholic Church to concern and compassion for the victims. An educated laity has replaced the superstitious medieval masses, says Doyle, and will not tolerate a church that puts its image and influence over the welfare of the people. Thomas P. Doyle, an air force chaplain stationed in Europe, is one of three who drafted a ninety-two-page report on clergy sexual abuse that was given to the United States bishops in June 1985. The report was for the most part ignored.

As you read, consider the following questions:

1. According to the author, what is so threatening to Vatican bureaucrats and many bishops?
2. What does Doyle recommend the Catholic Church do to restore its credibility?

January 6, 2002, the day *The Boston Globe* published its first major story about the sex abuse cover-up, was the day the hurricane hit land, but it was not the beginning of the storm, nor was it the peak moment. The Boston storm has turned out to be a squall line reaching across the Catholic church. In January 2002, few would have believed the debacle would have lasted this long, but it has. And it shows no sign of letting up! More and more corruption and dishonesty is being dredged up. The anger has spread across all stripes of Catholics with the staunch orthodox as disgusted as the futuristic liberals.

Making Excuses

The hierarchical system still has plenty of defenders who keep repeating the same tired excuses like frightened children whistling in the dark. The two main targets for deflecting attention from the fundamental issue are, of course, the secular press and the homosexual establishment. Some quibble over the distinction between pedophiles and ephebophiles, laying the blame on a conspiracy between gays and the hedonistic critics of traditional Catholic morality. What these people don't get is the fact that sexual abuse is sexual abuse, whether the target is a 6-year-old boy or a 46-year-old woman, and when the abuser is a priest the evil is compounded with a gross betrayal of trust, which is tantamount to spiritual rape.

Probably one of the more ridiculous excuses has been to lay the blame on the so-called sexual revolution of the '60s and '70s. Cultural trends don't cause sexual disorders. Besides, there was plenty of abuse going on before then. The difference is that it was more deeply hidden, in part by a deep-seated Catholic naiveté that prevented the average Catholic or average anyone from believing that priests would do these things.

Members of the secular media have really taken their share of hits from the clerical establishment from the pope on down. The slams from people in the Vatican bureaucracy, the editors of *La Civiltà Cattolica* and various high-ranking churchmen throughout the world would be almost comical were it not for the fact that these arrogant pronouncements further victimize the victims by directly implying that this is all an exaggeration. *Civiltà*, an influential Jesuit journal, claims that the press' treatment of the sex scandal is "morbid and scandalous" and reflects growing anti-Catholicism in the United States. If they really think people believe that assessment, then it's fair to say that their grip on reality is tenuous at best. The coverage is certainly morbid and scandalous, because the sex abuse is morbid, and the arrogant cover-ups have been worse than scandalous. Anti-Catholic attitudes! They're right in principle but off the mark. Allowing the sexual pillaging of Catholic young people and then lying about it while at the same time squandering millions of Catholic dollars in hush money, that's anti-Catholic!

Several years ago Capuchin Fr. Michael Crosby wrote that the Catholic church is a dysfunctional family. All of the classic symptoms of dysfunction and addictive behavior are present. For years, clergy sexual abuse of children and adults was like the elephant in the living room. Everyone tiptoed around, and no one wanted to ask why it was there. Then the elephant moved, and the whole house shook.

It's fair to say that the catalogue of excuses offered by the leadership for its totally inadequate and irresponsible reaction to the many cases of abuse, and the attacks on the secular press, the so-called materialistic society, the plaintiffs' lawyers, the victims' rights advocates and even the victims themselves, are symptoms of a combination of corporate denial and fear.

A Problem with the Clerical System

This crisis is a massive deluge that didn't start in January 2002 or even back in 1985. It goes back for centuries. . . . The eruptions that have been taking place not only in the United States but throughout the world are indicative of the fact that more is wrong than sexually abusive clerics. There is something radically amiss with the entire clerical system. There are reasons why the church's leadership has acted as it did but these reasons are far from the hardly believable catalogue of excuses we keep hearing.

To have handled the problem effectively from the beginning would have necessitated a radical shift in attitude and outlook. In a sense this is a theological issue: Who is the church? The clerical establishment thinks that it is the church and guards its security at all costs. The denial mechanisms we have seen are indicative of a deep-seated fear that the structures, so long the fortress of the clerical sub-culture, will change. To have responded with immediate compassion and total concern for the victims carried with it the immense risk of losing the security provided by the power and prestige of the episcopate. This is the risk that goes with reaching out as Christ would have done. It means that the value of one victim goes far beyond all the power, prestige and monetary worth of the entire system.

Ignoring the Victims

A two-edged common denominator in the bizarre series of statements coming out of certain highly placed Vatican officials, Italian journals, prelates such as Cardinal Oscar Andrés Rodríguez Maradiago of Honduras and others is the narcissistic obsession with the image of the "church" and the scandalous lack of concern for the victims. Why? Simply put, it's because the prelates don't know the victims. The church is people, not rules, traditions, rituals or governmental structures. Some bishops have tried to justify their lawyers' incredible hardball tactics with victims by saying that they have an obligation to protect the church's patrimony. That's a church buzzword for the money. In other words, the money is more important than the horrific damage done to the victims by the abusing priests.

All that most of the victims ever wanted was belief, understanding and compassion from the bishops. Instead they got threats, intimidation, manipulation and subterfuge. The ecclesiastical establishment couldn't break free of the obsessive secrecy and self-absorption to take the risk of embracing the victims.

The Medieval Church Is Dying

Perhaps what is so threatening to the Vatican bureaucrats and many of the bishops is the realization that the medieval church is finally starting to crumble before them. This was the church that put so much stock in power, prestige and control. The masses were largely uneducated and superstitious. They had to be controlled because the hierarchy knew what was best for all, and the laity was generally in a state of sin anyway. It was easy to build kingdoms, little and big, in the church power structure.

American Catholics Critical, but Hopeful

Do you approve or disapprove of the way the Catholic Church has handled the issue of sexual abuse of children by priests?

23% Approve

71% Disapprove

Do you think the church can or cannot be trusted to handle this issue properly in the future?

59% Can be trusted

36% Cannot be trusted

ABC News–*Washington Post* Beliefnet Poll, *CQ Researcher*, May 3, 2002.

All one has to do is take an impartial look at the traditional governmental model, clearly outlined in the Code of Canon Law, to see the concept of monarchy loud and clear. That model doesn't work anymore! The false presumption of uneducated, sinful masses is a figment of history. The people, led by the abuse survivors, won't tolerate an institutional church that puts looking good and the preservation of power and control above the emotional and spiritual welfare of persons. The medieval church is dying, terminally afflicted with the virus called "clericalism."

This is all a painful reminder of the fact that the Catholic church is centered on Jesus Christ, not any human structure. Furthermore, its claims to reflect the word and example of Christ must be present in the real life of the church, not just in sermons or theology books. It means little to a wounded survivor to say "the church is love" unless we do it, not by word but by action.

Restoring Credibility

The credibility of the hierarchy will not be restored by mere words—more decrees, more public apologies, more promises of "no more abuse." New and streamlined ways of disposing of abusive clerics (and the further tromping underfoot of that wonderful American value called "due process") won't do it. The bishops need to openly and honestly admit why there have been cover-ups and lies. Following this, their credibility might possibly be restored somewhere in the future if they begin now to actually get to know the victims and survivors by reaching out, one by one, to them.

"What would Jesus Do?" That's not just a cutesy motto for teens or dreamy idealists. That is the fundamental issue before the church today. The answer is obvious. It's not one that comes out of power or medieval panoply but genuine compassion for those who are in pain. It means action, not just words. It also means accepting not only what Jesus would do, but quite possibly what he is doing right now, and that is reminding us just what his church is all about.

"There can be no internship, no probation period, no halfway ministry for a man guilty even one time of child sexual abuse."

The Catholic Church Must Institute a Zero-Tolerance Policy for Child Sexual Abuse

David McGrath

A priest who sexually abuses children betrays the Catholic family's trust and should be immediately terminated by the Catholic Church, writes David McGrath in the following viewpoint. Children are taught that priests have special powers and deserve the utmost respect and are thus reluctant to reveal abuse, argues McGrath. Moreover, he maintains, Catholic parents are proud, not suspicious, when a priest pays special attention to their child. A zero-tolerance policy is necessary, he argues, because one instance of betrayal ruins lives and destroys the trust that families place in men of God. McGrath is a writer and teaches writing and Native American literature at the College of DuPage, in Glen Ellyn, Illinois.

As you read, consider the following questions:
1. According to McGrath, why are some parents of child abuse victims tricked into sacrificing their children?
2. What did the priest in McGrath's account do to single out his child abuse victim?
3. In McGrath's opinion, what is the price a child pays for resistance to a priest?

As America's Catholic bishops gather in Dallas, Texas, June 13, 2002, to debate whether to institute a zero tolerance policy for priests who sexually abuse minors, they need to face a devastating truth. I am not referring to the odds that the offender will prey again; nor to the severity or duration of his offense; nor even to the measurable harm inflicted upon the victim. I am asking them to consider the egregious betrayal of a Catholic family's unquestioning trust in a man of God.

Any member of the clergy or the legal profession who doesn't see that as yet another compelling reason for immediate termination has only to speak with the parents of abuse victims—parents racked with guilt for having trusted too much. Like "marks" who eagerly handed their money over to a con artist, some parents let themselves be tricked into sacrificing their children because of their blind devotion to the church.

One such case involved "William" (names and places have been changed at the subject's request), who was sexually molested by a priest three decades ago. The abuse, which consisted mainly of fondling, went on for at least two years.

A Friend of the Family

William said the priest had been a friend of his parents for as long as he could remember. He was a pastor at a parish near Dubuque, Iowa, but he would often visit the family when he was in Chicago. His parents thought they were blest to have a priest as a special friend. They hadn't gone to college, and they saw Father Mark as a repository of knowledge and culture and sophisticated humor. He gave them an illusion of privileged connection as he shared with them jokes about the bishops and cardinals and celebrities with whom he sometimes mingled.

Father Mark would write letters that his mother would study and reread, sending William downstairs for the dictionary to learn what Father meant when he said he was "edified" after his last trip to the Vatican. She and William's father seldom failed to mention their "friend, Father Mark" in conversation.

Back then William hadn't figured out what Father Mark

derived from their family, though it seemed as if the priest acted as if he were his godfather. He was always sending him presents, writing him letters, teaching him things. William was proud of how Father had singled him out, and his brothers and friends were envious.

When Father Mark visited, William's parents went all out, turning the house over to him. It was, his mother would say, like having Jesus himself visit. And when his mother and father slept on a cot and couch so that Father Mark could have the privacy of their bedroom, they were touched by the priest's willingness to help with the family accommodations when he'd offer to let William sleep with him in the big bed.

A New Understanding Mandates a New Policy

We should be targeting on systemic rather than surface solutions.

The public disclosure of reassignments within the system of a Boston priest—a known pedophile—to pastoral ministry triggered the present crisis. There were multiple complaints, multiple reassignments and multiple instances of child molestation. The system provided medical, psychological and pastoral care for the perpetrator, but apparently did not at that time recognize pedophilia as an incurable mental illness that fixates erotic attraction on prepubescent children. Nor, it seems, did the system acknowledge that pedophilia is in all cases a crime. Systemic breakdown on these two fronts is not likely to reoccur.

The illness is incurable. The sick priest must be barred from all unsupervised contact with children. The crime must be reported and, the cardinals are saying, there is no place for a pedophile in ecclesiastical ministry.

William Byron, *Origins*, May 16, 2002.

Did William's parents mean well? Was that reason for them to be suspicious? And why wouldn't William tell his own mother about what the priest did behind the closed door?

In addition to this parental unconditional imprimatur of the priest, there was an even stronger force of authority. An 8-year-old, especially one enrolled in a Catholic elementary school 30 years ago, still straddles the threshold between fantasy and reality. Bible stories have him imagining demons wearing lascivious smiles perched on his left shoulder, and white clad angels displaying disapproving frowns on his right. He's mesmerized by stories of Lourdes and Fatima and Guadalupe, and each night is prepared to welcome his very own vision, its evanescence framed by his darkened bedroom window.

He is taught that priests have special access to the preternatural universe, since they know the magic words that turn bread and wine into Christ's body and blood. William's school teacher, Sister Elizabeth, tells the New Testament stories of the emergence and power of priests, explains that they're Jesus's surrogates on earth. So it's practically a sin not to stand when a priest enters the classroom for religious instruction or to keep your eyes open while receiving the good Father's blessing before he leaves. Being chosen by one of them as a particular friend was for William both a miracle and a sacred vocation. The boy's only chance for deliverance from this predatory evil was his family; yet their "good" intentions made them blind to the danger.

Think of an 8-year-old facing corporal punishment, parental disapproval and eternal damnation—all a painful price to pay for any resistance to the good Father. So William never told his parents, never told anyone. And even though decades have past, the priest is dead, and media attention and societal empathy have made it possible for victims to unburden themselves, William keeps his secret. He smothers the grenade of that awful truth, he says, to protect his aging parents.

Doctors who purposely poison their patients: Should we give them another chance? Pilots who fly drunk just one time . . . it's clear where I'm going. There can be no internship, no probation period, no halfway ministry for a man guilty even one time of child sexual abuse. One time is ruinous. One time is a sledgehammer that cracks lives, faiths, trusts, families and children. Forever.

4

*"The adoption of an absolute policy might
provide needed relief but it could also lead
to further abuse."*

Zero Tolerance of Child Sexual Abuse Could Lead to Further Abuse

National Catholic Reporter

Zero-tolerance policies impose severe penalties for first-time offenses. According to the editors of the *National Catholic Reporter* in the following viewpoint, zero tolerance of priests who sexually abuse children may lead to further abuse because the important question—why priests were allowed to abuse children in the first place—will not be answered. The church will only find productive solutions if bishops are willing to allow outside examination, the authors maintain. Moreover, they claim, simplistic solutions based on unsupported claims may lead to dangerous policies that do not prevent child sexual abuse. The *National Catholic Reporter* is an independent Catholic newsweekly.

As you read, consider the following questions:

1. What do the authors believe pains Catholics more than dealing with the clergy abuse issue?
2. According to the authors, what upsets and discourages ordinary Catholics about the way bishops operate?
3. What idea held by some Catholic prelates do the authors find disturbing?

National Catholic Reporter, "Solutions That Make Matters Worse," *National Catholic Reporter*, vol. 38, May 10, 2002, pp. 24–28. Copyright © 2002 by *National Catholic Reporter*. Reproduced by permission.

Facing a widespread uprising of Catholic laity and a relentless media, the U.S. bishops seem to be edging toward the adoption of a "zero-tolerance policy" for clergy sex abuse at their June 2002 meeting. As Pope John Paul II said in April 2002 to the American cardinals in Rome, there is no place in the priesthood for those who would harm the young. Looking ahead, it makes sense for the bishops not to equivocate on clergy abuse. Catholic parents need assurances their children will be safe.

Taking a Wiser Course

However, when it comes to accusations dating back many years or even decades, the bishops might be wiser to study each case on its own merits.

The adoption of an absolute policy might provide needed relief but it could also lead to further abuse. Would it serve the interests of the Catholic community or that community's sense of justice to enforce the most severe punishment for a priest who may have acted in an improper manner many years ago but who has since established a clean record? Crimes need to be treated as crimes, but there are well-established reasons in Western law for statutes of limitations. The wiser course may be to scrutinize each case carefully. We worry about policies enacted under pressure that end up devoid of human assessment and the need to make distinctions in acts or patterns of human behavior.

While we have persistently pressed for more hierarchical accountability in this area, we also fear that a simplistic one-size-fits-all policy will end up in the future looking a lot like the notoriously failed "three strikes and you're out" policy [in which a person convicted of a "serious" or "violent" felony for the third time serves a life sentence] that has filled U.S. prisons in recent years.

The Role of the Bishops

A deeper problem with the discussions—or rather, lack of discussions—in recent weeks has been the episcopal focus on how fast and under what circumstance to throw out priests. They are missing a crucial point. As pained as Catholics are in dealing with the clergy abuse issue, they are even more pained by the failure of their bishops to protect their children. They are being forced to acknowledge unbelievable patterns of cover-up and denial that persisted over decades. Catholics are looking for answers. They are demanding accountability.

In this light, the Vatican meeting in April 2002, which did not address the role of the bishops in the scandal, is being viewed by many as the latest incident in a longer pattern of denial. It now looks like the pattern will extend to the U.S. bishops' June 2002 meeting. Short of a thorough episcopal self-examination coupled with serious efforts to open up and involve the laity in future discussions, the bishops seem to be making matters worse. They are certainly not showing evidence that they grasp the seriousness of the moment. Nor are they indicating that they yet have what it takes to lead the church to restored health.

An Ineffective Policy

Zero tolerance has evolved into one of those squishy catch-all phrases that makes us feel good because it gives the appearance that something is being done. It cloaks us in the false sense that the problem is being solved. . . .

In terms of the church, a zero-tolerance policy would be ineffectual if it placed the spotlight solely on predatory priests and diverted it from the church's culture of secrecy.

Dawn Turner Trice, *Chicago Tribune*, June 13, 2002.

If the June 2002 sessions are dominated by "zero-tolerance" discussions, the bishops will have once more avoided the truly pressing questions at hand, chief among them: What allowed this to happen in the first place? To answer this question and many others related to it requires a commitment to openness and inclusion that the church has not seen in a long time. It is the closed atmosphere in which the bishops operate, it is their unwillingness to allow themselves to be assessed from the outside that upsets and discourages ordinary Catholics.

If the bishops do not open up the discussions, they cannot reestablish trust. If the bishops do not allow outsiders to walk with them, to work with them, to help them define the problems at hand, they are almost certainly not going to find solutions that will help move the church forward. Without major changes in attitude toward the laity, any solutions the bishops come up with will be considered skeptically.

The Danger of Simplistic Solutions

Without properly framing the problems, solutions are likely to be simplistic. Worse, they can lead to dangerous and even injurious thinking. We find, for example, very disturbing that some Catholic prelates are now floating the idea of rooting out gays from the Catholic clergy and forbidding young gay Catholics from becoming priests. The not-so-subtle implication here is that gay priests are more inclined than heterosexual priests to act out their sexuality. No supporting evidence is offered to back up the claim.

Cardinal Anthony J. Bevilacqua of Philadelphia has raised this flag. He stated in April 2002 that gays are not suitable for the priesthood, even if they remain celibate. His explanation was that they do not give up family and marriage, as heterosexuals are required. According to Bevilacqua, what the gay candidate for the priesthood gives up is "what the church considers an aberration, a moral evil."

All such talk will do is muddy the picture, not provide any clarity and it will provide convenient scapegoats. Far more responsible commentators have already noted the need to discuss the implications of increasing numbers of homosexuals in the clergy ranks. Such discussions would be valuable if they are approached honestly and in the spirit of learning and helping, not seeking vengeance against those of a certain sexual orientation.

In real terms, a purge of gay priests is highly unlikely. Any such effort would quickly lead to a frenzy of finger-pointing. We concur with Bishop Thomas Gumbleton, an auxiliary bishop of the Detroit archdiocese, who said that these kinds of statements contradict existing church policy. "All homosexual persons have a right to be welcomed into the community, to hear the word of God, and to receive pastoral care," the U.S. bishops wrote in a 1997 pastoral message to the parents of homosexual children. Said Gumbleton, "I don't know how we could tell parents to accept their children and then we won't accept them."

Finally, it is important to remember that our priests and bishops are hurting, perhaps as never before. It is tragic that the Catholic clergy, filled with men who have given their lives for the service of others, is being so tarnished.

Lay voices are proliferating. This is a healthy sign and needs to be encouraged. The widespread calls by laity for episcopal accountability might also be seen by the hierarchy as a sign of growth and health. Most laypeople speaking out and getting involved are doing so in attempts to heal and in response to the need for greater unity among clergy and laity alike.

> *"Based on the fact that 90% of the incidents [of child sexual abuse] involve young boys, we should probably be using the term, 'homosexual predators.'"*

The Catholic Church Should Ban Homosexuals from the Priesthood

Tom Barrett

In the following viewpoint, Tom Barrett argues that child sexual abuse in the Catholic Church is rooted in the training and ordaining of homosexual priests. Barrett asserts that evidence shows that homosexuals are more likely than heterosexuals to be pedophiles. The only way the Catholic Church can protect its children, he argues, is to immediately expel homosexual priests. Barrett is an ordained minister, author, and editor of *Conservative Truth*, an e-mail newsletter that focuses on moral and political issues from a biblical viewpoint.

As you read, consider the following questions:

1. What two reasons does Barrett give to support his claim that a shortage of priests is a poor excuse for ordaining homosexuals?
2. What biblical evidence does the author give to support his position that God condemns homosexuality?
3. What does Barrett claim is the sin committed by the leaders of the Catholic Church?

The Catholic Church is in serious trouble. It has paid out over a billion dollars in legal costs and settlements for cases involving 600 pedophile priests. Everyone, from wet-behind-the-ears reporters to District Attorneys, is giving the Pope advice on how to fix the problem. But, curiously, no one wants to talk about the real problem, the secret that is at the root of the pedophile problem.

Revealing the Real Secret

"But I thought pedophile priests were the secret," some would say. Well, if that is the secret, it's been an open secret for quite a while. No, the problem lies much deeper, and is going to be much more difficult to deal with than the relatively small percentage of pedophile priests who have been identified.

Others might feel that the Catholic Church's secret is the way it has been able to use its strength to control local governments. Cardinal Bernard Law of Boston has been criticized in all the news media for protecting the molesters of 130 boys from the authorities. The District Attorney of Philadelphia has finally admitted publicly that for decades, whenever there was a complaint about a priest molesting little boys, it was routinely turned over to the Archbishop instead of allowing the police to investigate. Can you imagine that kind of treatment for a Protestant minister, a Jewish rabbi, or for that matter clergy of any other religion? But that is not the secret of which I speak.

Much has been made of the willingness of Cardinals and Bishops to hide not only the illegal actions of priests, but also the priests themselves, from the police. Documents subpoenaed from the Archdiocese of Massachusetts reveal that pedophiles have routinely been moved from one unsuspecting parish to another. Some Catholic leaders even went to the point of establishing "safe houses," much like the CIA uses, where rogue priests could be hidden to avoid arrest. Protecting the image of the Catholic Church was more important to these supposed men of God than protecting children from predatory beasts. Speaking of people like this, Jesus said in Luke 17:2, "It would be better for him if a stone was tied around his neck and he be thrown into the sea than to offend one of these little ones." As reprehensible as these actions have been, they are only a symptom of the real problem. The secret lies deeper.

"Ah," you say, "I know what you're talking about. Celibacy. It's unnatural. Celibacy is what is causing these priests to prey on innocent children!" Not at all. Abstaining from all sexual activity other than heterosexual marriage is clearly a Biblical requirement for any minister. However celibacy is not a requirement for ministry. I am a happily married minister myself, and my wife has helped me be more effective in my ministry. As a matter of fact, for over 1200 years the Roman Catholic Church allowed its priests and bishops to marry. Thirty-nine of the popes were married. However, the Bible is clear that celibacy is a good thing, a gift that God gives to certain people. It is certainly not the reason that some priests prey rather than pray. We must dig deeper to discover the secret that has caused so many so much pain.

Warning! We are now entering politically incorrect territory. If you are terrified by the prospect of rocking the boat, going against the status quo, or discussing ideas that would bring you to the attention of the PC Police, stop reading now.

The secret to which I refer attacks the very foundation of the Catholic Church, its moral base. The secret is that the Catholic Church has knowingly accepted homosexuals into its priesthood for decades. In January of 2000, the *Kansas City Star* created a stir by claiming that Catholic priests were dying of AIDS at four times the rate of the general population. The Catholic Church responded by saying the percentage was not nearly that high. But that is not the point. With a celibate clergy, there should be no priests dying of AIDS.

Why Ordain Homosexuals?

Why are Catholic Seminaries training and ordaining known homosexuals? The most frequent excuse is that there is a severe shortage of priests, with many parishes closing because of a lack of clergy. This is a poor excuse on two counts. First, many straight men decide against the priesthood because of the predominance of homosexuals. I watched an interview on CBS News with a professor of philosophy at a Catholic college. He stated that he dropped out of Seminary because

A Story of Homosexual Seduction

Priestly pedophilia *is very much a homosexual issue*. The Fall River Diocese's infamous Fr. James Porter committed many depredations, all against young boys. Boston's Fr. John Geoghan is said to have preyed exclusively on boys. Of the 87 priests whose names were turned over to prosecutors for having one or more incidents of pedophilia on their records, at most one or two are accused of molesting girls, but along with boys as well. A priest from Gloucester who retired because of a bad heart six months ago was picked up by police and charged with soliciting sex from young boys. Christopher Reardon, the Youth Minister at St. Agnes in Middleton, was convicted of molesting boys. Fr. George Spagnolia in Lowell, the priest who was fighting his dismissal for alleged molestation and refusing to leave his rectory, claimed that he had always been celibate, even during his nearly 20 years of leave from the priesthood. However, the press dug up a "lover" from the time of his leave, later confirmed by Fr. Spagnolia. You didn't really need to read on to know that Fr. Spagnolia's "lover" was a man, not a woman. Yes, the molestations and sexual seductions are routinely of a homosexual nature.

Pedophilia is not about unequal access to boys. Altar girls have been in the Massachusetts Archdiocese for quite some time. Catholic schools usually have slightly more girls than boys. Priests who act as youth ministers interact with both boys and girls. But the pedophiles are not preying on the girls. It is the boys who are targeted. The predators are males molesting and violating boys, which makes this a homosexual issue. Indeed, the *National Catholic Register* recently reported that psychiatrist Richard Fitzgibbons "said that virtually every priest he's treated who has sexually abused children had previously been involved in homosexual relationships with other adults."

C. Thomas Fitzpatrick, *New Oxford Review*, June 2002.

he was uncomfortable with the number of homosexuals both among students and teachers. An article by Father David Trosch states, "A leading American churchman is claiming that the Roman Catholic priesthood has become 'primarily a gay culture' that deters heterosexual men from taking up vocations. In his book, *The Changing Face of the Priesthood*, Father Donald Cozzens says that an exodus of experienced priests from the church, many of them to marry, has drastically altered the gay-straight ratio. 'At issue at the beginning of the 21st century is the growing perception that the priesthood is, or is becoming, a gay profession,' Cozzens writes. 'Heterosexual seminarians are made uncomfortable by the number of gays around them.'"

The second reason the shortage of priests is a poor excuse for ordaining homosexuals is that there are over twenty thousand ordained Catholic priests in this country who are not allowed to serve in parishes. That's one out of every three priests! These are the priests who have married. They are still ordained, but because the Roman Catholic hierarchy changed the rules 800 years ago, married priests are not allowed to serve as parish priests. So we have a situation where the Catholic Church refuses the services of men whose lives are in harmony with the Word of God (Paul the Apostle said that a bishop should be "the husband of one wife"), while welcoming homosexual men whose lifestyles are in direct contradiction to the Word of God.

Some apologists for allowing homosexuals to serve as priests claim that a homosexual can have that sexual orientation, but remain chaste. That is no doubt true. But a survey of homosexual priests revealed that "73% of them said that they were sexually active either frequently or occasionally."

How prevalent is homosexuality among Catholic priests? Father David C. Trosch writes, "Shortly after ordination I had reflected that it would be terrible that if as many as 2% of priests were homosexual. Perhaps a year later in a conversation with a highly placed priest of the archdiocese he stated that approximately 35% of priests were homosexuals. It was most disconcerting to read the following article in which Father Donald Cozzens, the head of a Catholic seminary, says that estimates range as high as 60% of American priests are homosexual. Unfortunately the article states that, 'Cozzens . . . concedes some bishops and even some popes may have been gay.'"

A Moral Lapse

What has caused the Catholic leadership to accept homosexuals as priests? The Catholic Church, along with many other institutions, has been affected by the loose morals of the last thirty years. Political correctness proclaims that everything is OK as long as it feels good. It has become unfashionable, almost a capital offense, to utter "homosexual" and "sin" in the same sentence. It was during this time that the flood of homosexuals into the Catholic priesthood began. Is anyone surprised that most of the revelations of priests molesting and raping small children are coincidental with this loss of a moral base?

I can almost hear the howls of outrage as I write this. "Homophobe! Reactionary! Right-wing religious extremist! Don't you know that pedophiles molest little girls, too?" Of course I do. But I also know that the vast majority of pedophiles are only attracted to little boys. In fact, the use of the term "pedophiles" to describe the sins of these priests, while politically correct, is misleading. Based on the fact that 90% of the incidents involve young boys, we should probably be using the term, "homosexual predators." I often hear the homosexual lobby state that homosexuals are no more likely to be pedophiles than straight men. That is a lie straight from hell. According to Leonard Kennedy, "Dr. Judith Reisman, using 1992 statistics, has calculated that, per capita, homosexual men abuse boys fifty times as frequently as other men abuse girls."

Of course, you will never hear about these facts from the mainstream press. But surprisingly, a Vatican spokesman interviewed by *The Catholic News Service* admits that, "Most publicized cases of sex abuse by clergy against minors have involved homosexual acts." He also said he ". . .did not want to draw more attention to this topic, especially while U.S. church leaders were dealing with the more immediate problem of sex abuse by clergy."

I realize that the majority of Catholics are good, moral people who are as outraged by this scandal as any of the talking heads on TV. In fact, they feel more outrage, because their leaders have betrayed them. When I speak of the sins of the Catholic Church, I am speaking of the cowardice and pride of many of its leaders, not the Catholics who attend Mass every Sunday hoping to find a moral foundation on which to build their lives. Of course that moral foundation Catholic parishioners seek is the Bible. And it is the Bible, the very Word of God, which many of the Cardinals and Bishops have spat upon and trampled underfoot.

A Bible Lesson

"How can you say that, Tom? These leaders revere the Bible. They have based their lives upon it." Really? Then how can they allow homosexuals, whose lifestyle the Bible deplores, to flood their seminaries and spread their evil message to unsuspecting parishioners around the world? In a survey of openly homosexual priests, says Kennedy, "They admitted that their dissenting views are passed on to their parishioners and penitents. Only 9% said that they advise the faithful to follow the teaching of the Church in sexual matters."

It's time for a Bible lesson. Leviticus 20:13 says, "If a man lies with a man as one lies with a woman, both of them have done what is detestable. They must be put to death." God is very clear in His condemnation of homosexuality. By the way, the same chapter puts incest and bestiality in the same category as homosexual sin.

Moving to the New Testament, Paul the Apostle in Romans 1:27 talks about men who, ". . . abandoned natural relations with women and were inflamed with lust for one another. Men committed indecent acts with other men, and received in themselves the due penalty for their perversion." Never one to mince words, Paul goes on in I Corinthians 6:9 to say, "Do you not know that the wicked will not inherit the kingdom of God? Do not be deceived: Neither the sexually immoral nor idolaters nor adulterers nor prostitutes nor homosexuals."

God is very clear in His Word about what is natural and good, as well as what is unnatural and perverted. What about these verses (and dozens of similar Bible references) is so hard for the Catholic Church's hierarchy to understand?

Now I am going to step on some toes. It is easy to criticize Paul Shanley, the priest who helped found NAMBLA (the North American Man-Boy Love Association), who advocated sex between adults and little boys, and who put his words into actions. Likewise, everyone stands up and cheers when Cardinal Law of Massachusetts, who covered up for Shanley and other homosexual predators for decades, is asked to resign. Men such as these are easy targets for our outrage.

The Sins of Catholic Leaders

But where is the outrage over the sin committed by the highest leaders of the Catholic Church when they made the conscious decision to ordain men whom the Bible refers to as "perverted?" If a homosexual had been admitted to the Bible College I attended, the president would have been fired. Bible Colleges and Seminaries have an obligation to make sure their graduates are people committed to teaching the Bible in its purity. Why then do the members of the Catholic Church, as well as many liberal Protestant denominations, stand by like sheep while their leaders afflict them with clergy whose lifestyle is an affront to everything the Bible teaches?

When the pope called the American cardinals to Rome to discuss the problems here, it took them two days to come up with a "Zero-Tolerance" policy toward pedophilia. As one TV commentator on *MSNBC* pointed out, "I don't know why they had to come up with more rules. They already have it in their rulebook. It's called the Bible." They could have saved thousands of dollars in airfare and limos.

Lest my readers leave this article with the opinion that I, a Protestant, am bashing the Catholic Church, let me quote a prominent Catholic theologian. "In a lengthy article in the November 2000 issue of the magazine *The Catholic World Report*, published in San Francisco, Father Paul Shaughnessy says that, 'in a sociological sense, any institution that has lost the capacity to mend itself on its own initiative and by its own resources, an institution that is unable to uncover and expel its own miscreants, is corrupt.' Shaughnessy then accuses the episcopacy in the United States, and the majority of religious orders, of being corrupt as defined sociologically."

I am not against Catholics. Most Catholics I know are good, moral people. I am definitely against any person or institution that makes it easy for predators to damage our precious little ones. Jesus refers to His children as sheep, because we need protection. Ministers are supposed to be shepherds who protect the flock. When the shepherd becomes a wolf, he needs to be removed, and put into a cage from which he can no longer devastate the sheep. He should never be moved to another unsuspecting flock.

Let us all pray for the leaders who have allowed such horrible things to take place. We need to pray that they will repent, and resign from the positions they hold. And we need to pray that those who replace them will clean up the homosexual subculture that threatens to take over the Catholic Church. The Vatican is discussing keeping homosexuals out of Seminaries in the future. That is not enough. All homosexual priests must be expelled immediately. That is the only way the Catholic Church can purge itself of this terrible malignancy. Please join me in praying that the leaders of the Catholic Church will stop looking the other way and deal forcefully with this issue.

"[Celibacy] may, in some circumstances, incubate men who will lead tragic double lives behind its screen."

The Catholic Church Should Reevaluate Its Celibacy Requirement for Priests

Eugene Cullen Kennedy

According to his research, writes Eugene Cullen Kennedy in the following viewpoint, many priests do not view celibacy as a virtue but as a condition to which they must adjust. Unfortunately, he maintains, immature candidates for the priesthood are not yet aware of their own sexuality and may later become confused and tortured by sexual conflict. If a priest is particularly disturbed, says Kennedy, he may eventually sexually abuse children. Kennedy, a former priest, is a professor of psychology at Loyola University in Chicago and author of the book *The Unhealed Wound: The Church and Human Sexuality*.

As you read, consider the following questions:
1. What did Kennedy's research reveal about how priests live celibate lives?
2. How does celibacy serve the institution of the Catholic Church, in the author's view?
3. According to Kennedy, what happens when priests act out their sexual conflicts?

C elibacy is not in itself the cause of pedophilia in Catholic priests any more than marriage is the cause of divorce among married people. Both, however, are psychological states that only seem easy to understand. The motives people have for entering each state may not always be healthy, causing pain and heartache to more than the person making the choice.

Marriage appears so appropriate, so right, so to speak, for humans that it seems an almost natural institution. Yet marriage has been, and is, understood in almost contradictory ways across the cultures of the world. In some, it is a choice of the heart made by individuals, while in others, it is arranged by parents and therefore an act of obedience. To some, its only and overriding purpose is to stabilize the relationship in which children are born into the world. Others view it as ordered to the fulfillment and friendship that men and women seek so deeply in life.

The motives for marriage do not always match these varied ideals and the state may yield as much pain as it does happiness. The failure rate is high. And yet most people want to, and do, get married. Many of them learn, long after they have forgotten the words of their vows, that they never really knew either themselves or the person they married.

Understanding Celibacy

Celibacy refers to an unmarried state. Chastity is something different: it applies to the unmarried and married alike, asking them to be faithful to a religious vow or to a spouse, respectively. Celibacy's history in the Roman Catholic Church is more of a discipline, as it is described, than a virtue, as it is promoted. It was introduced ten centuries after Jesus chose a married man to head his church, in order to prevent priests from handing on lands to their descendants.

While it can be understood as a voluntary choice made by people who want to give their whole lives in service to a community larger than their own family, it is, in practice, not free but a condition that must be accepted by young men who wish to be priests. During their training, the seminarians of years past typically learned of celibacy's possibilities of glory and the example of the saints who surrender marriage to serve the Lord.

In reality, however, celibacy is a complex and subtle state. It may attract those aspiring to heroic virtue, but may also attract large numbers of persons with very different motivations. In a national study of American priests conducted for the American bishops, my research attempted to determine how priests regarded and lived this condition of celibacy.

Luckovich. © 2002 by *Atlanta Journal-Constitution*. Reprinted by permission of Creators Syndicate, Inc.

We learned that even the healthiest priests in the sample did not perceive celibacy as a virtue to be practiced as much as a condition of life to which they had to adjust. This required an enormous investment of energy and often led them to do things—such as taking expensive vacations, having big cars, or costly hobbies—for which they were criticized. Other less healthy priests in the sample accepted celibacy for reasons varied and emotionally self-serving enough to raise questions about how sturdy a foundation it is for ministry.

An Unexpected Adjustment

Even then, many immature candidates found no challenge in celibacy because their own sexuality had not yet awakened within them and had not yet been integrated into their personality development. Because they were not attracted to marriage, celibacy was never a true existential choice for them. Often, their sexual feelings only asserted themselves after they had entered parish work. They were dismayed and puzzled by erotic attractions to boys that reflected their own pre-adolescent state. Celibacy for these men was an illusion of virtue, a stage set for life rather than a condition for service, and they found themselves abusing the trust that this presumed virtue won for them by seducing and defiling the innocent in their care. Their lack of maturity was reflected in their low-level denial and distorted descriptions of their behavior.

The more disturbed the priest, the more disturbed was the sexual adjustment he forged under the cover a celibate priesthood provided. It became apparent that celibacy existed far more for the purposes of the institution than the growth of seminarians or the good of the people. Celibacy sealed an all-male clergy totally dependent on the institutional church for identity and livelihood. While we all admire men and women who voluntarily choose, with full understanding of themselves and the sacrifice they make, to lead celibate lives, we must not look away from the high price this requirement exacts from the large majority of even healthy persons.

While celibacy obviously does not cause pedophilia, it provides a setting and a shield for candidates whose lack of inner maturity dilutes celibacy as both a challenge and a choice. It may, in some circumstances, incubate men who will lead tragic double lives behind its screen. All too often, it has provided an *as if* life of virtue for men deeply entangled in and tortured by sexual conflicts. When they act out these conflicts, they cause others misery whose measure we are just beginning to take.

The possibilities of celibacy as a freely chosen state of service are overshadowed by the documented realities of celibacy as a forced condition of becoming a clergyman in service to an institution. It is late in the day for popes to do what they have refused to do, despite the obvious evidence of celibacy as a problematic state: examine celibacy in depth for the sake of both their priests and their people.

> "*Abuse by priests is a subset of a much larger and pervasive problem of child victimization.*"

Factors Other than Celibacy and Homosexuality Foster Child Sexual Abuse by Priests

Joseph J. Guido

Celibacy and homosexuality are not the cause of child sexual abuse within the Catholic Church, writes Joseph J. Guido in the following viewpoint. Most people who sexually abuse children are not priests, he maintains, so the discipline of celibacy is not likely the cause of the abuse. Moreover, research reveals that factors other than sexual orientation motivate the child sexual abuser, argues Guido. Guido is an assistant professor of psychology and a counseling psychologist at Providence College, in Rhode Island.

As you read, consider the following questions:

1. In Guido's opinion, what does the research on human sexuality he cites imply about the sexual abuse of children by priests?
2. What does Guido claim distinguishes pedophilia from other disorders?
3. According to the author, what two questions do survivors of sexual abuse pose?

The trial of John J. Geoghan, a former priest of the Archdiocese of Boston who is alleged to have molested more than 100 children, has been a distressing reminder that sexual abuse is committed by priests. It has also been a goad to action. Under pressure from the media and, in turn, civil authorities, the archdiocese has turned over to district attorneys the names of other priests against whom accusations have been made and has instituted a zero-tolerance policy with respect to future accusations. In doing so, it has served as a model for dioceses from Manchester, New Hampshire, to Los Angeles, California. It has been a trying time for everyone involved and a test of faith for some, and served as a desert few of us would choose to enter but into which the church has been led.

Yet under the press of crisis, perspective has been compromised at points. Some in the media have suggested that clerical celibacy and the particular culture that it engenders is the underlying disorder, of which sexual abuse is but the most egregious symptom. Others, in Rome and at the Vatican, have been quoted as saying that this is an American problem or that it is evidence that a homosexual orientation is incompatible with the ordained priesthood. While the temptation to fix blame is understandable, yielding to it in these ways serves no good purpose and can distract from the need to understand and remedy a crisis that has caused untold suffering to victims and that threatens the lived experience of the priesthood. It may be more helpful, therefore, to understand the sexual abuse of children by priests within the broader context of child victimization, to measure the American experience against the experience of the church elsewhere and to make important and informed distinctions in the delicate and complex matter of sexual orientation.

The Sexual Abuse of Children

One of the largest and most scientifically reputable studies of human sexuality was conducted by Edward O. Laumann, John H. Gagnon, Robert T. Michael and Stuart Michaels and published by the University of Chicago Press in 1994 as *The Social Organization of Sexuality*. Based on interviews and surveys of 3,432 American adults, it covers the gamut of sexual behaviors and experiences and is now generally regarded as a standard reference.

What Laumann and his colleagues discovered is that sexual abuse of children is disturbingly common: 17 percent of women and 12 percent of men report that they were abused before they reached puberty by an adolescent or adult, and the majority of them reported that the abuse was repeated. Girls were most at risk of being abused by adult men and adolescent males, while boys stood a greater risk from adolescent women, followed by adolescent males and men. What girls and boys share is a heightened risk of being abused by someone known to them. Only 7 percent reported being abused by a stranger, while 52 percent reported abuse by a relative and 29 percent by a family friend.

This research has two implications for understanding the sexual abuse of children by priests. First, abuse by priests is a subset of a much larger and pervasive problem of child victimization. It is unlikely, therefore, that clerical celibacy itself is a causative factor, when the vast majority of children who are abused are abused by those who are not priests. Second, priest abusers are likely to fit the pattern of those who abuse generally: they are known, trusted and familiar figures in the lives of the children they abuse. This suggests that the effects of abuse by a priest, as by a parent, sibling or babysitter, are the more serious because of the breach of trust they involve, and that perhaps for some priest abusers the priesthood is attractive precisely because it ensures relatively unfettered access to children, as does teaching, coaching and parenting. In effect, what distinguishes abusers of children is that they abuse, not specifically the fact that they are priests, parents or coaches.

The American Experience

The publicity that has surrounded the sexual abuse of children by priests in the United States, and to a lesser extent in Ireland, Australia and Great Britain, might lead one to suspect that if it is not an American problem per se, it is certainly one that has greater relevance for the English-speaking world. Research suggests, however, that the sexual abuse of children by priests is a problem for the church everywhere.

Indeed, what may differentiate one local experience from another is not the fact of clerical abuse but how prepared superiors are to respond to it appropriately.

In the summer of 2001, I conducted a survey of 81 religious superiors of a major clerical order, among them curial officials, provincials, vicars and formators. The vast majority (83 percent) of North American superiors were aware of accusations of sexual abuse against one of their priests, but so too were 43 percent of the superiors in Central America and the Caribbean, and approximately a third of the superiors in Africa, Asia/Pacific, Europe and South America. It could well be the case, therefore, that the North American experience differs from experience elsewhere more by degree than direction. If so, it might suggest that where policies and procedures for responding to allegations are not yet in place, the church would do well to develop them and so ensure that victims, the accused and the church itself will be cared for in the best way possible.

Two related findings are also of interest. First, in every region of the world except North America, superiors were more likely to be aware of sexual misconduct by a priest with an adult than they were of misconduct with a child; in North America, superiors were as likely to be aware of one as the other. Second, superiors everywhere are aware that some of their brother priests and religious were victims of sexual abuse as a child. Yet even here, policy lags behind knowledge. Relatively few superiors can rely upon established procedures for responding to allegations of clerical misconduct with adults, or for ensuring that their own brothers can receive the care and healing that they may require.

Homosexual Orientation Versus Pedophilia

Given the publicity about priests who have abused young males, it is understandable that some may be led to assume that a homosexual orientation is more likely to be associated with sexual abuse of a child. But this is an assumption that needs to be challenged. Pedophilia is distinguished by the fact that a person is attracted to a child as an object of sexual desire. It is the age of the child, not the child's gender, that specifies the disorder. Often pedophiles will abuse children of both genders. Thus, sexual orientation as commonly understood is secondary to the dominance of a disordered attraction to prepubescent children. Pedophiles who are attracted to boys and those who are attracted to girls have more in common with each other than they do with homosexuals and heterosexuals generally.

Pedophilia: A Complex Sexual Disorder

Pedophilia encompasses simple voyeurism of nude children, observing children at various stages of undress or assisting them to undress, sexual fondling, exposing oneself, performing oral sex on children and/or requesting them to return oral sex, or mutual masturbation. In most cases (except those involving incest), pedophiles do not require sexual penetration, and do not force their attentions on a child. They instead rely on guile, persuasion, and friendship, often displaying great tenderness and affection toward the child of their desire. Once a person has engaged in sexual activity with a child, he or she is then additionally labeled a "child molester." Thus, child molestation is subsumed in the overall condition of pedophilia.

A psychological profile of pedophilia escapes development because perpetrators appear to constitute a heterogenous group. However, some common characteristics prevail among both pedophiles and child molesters. The great majority of pedophiles are male, and they may be heterosexual, homosexual, or bisexual in orientation. Preference for children as sex partners may not be exclusive, and more often than not, pedophiles have no gender preference in prepubescent children. However, by a margin greater than two to one, most victims are girls. Moreover, the pedophile is usually a relative, friend, or neighbor of the child's family. Alcohol is associated with almost 50 percent of molestation cases, but is not necessarily correlated with pedophilia in general. Pedophilia tends to be a chronic condition, and recidivism is high.

Lauri R. Harding, *Gale Encyclopedia of Psychology*, 2nd ed., 2001.

A somewhat different pattern is evident when the child is an adolescent and postpubescent. An adult's sexual attraction to an adolescent, referred to as ephebophilia, shows a more decided preference for one gender over the other and, in this limited sense, parallels sexual orientation. Yet it would be unfair to infer from this that gay men who are priests are—because of their sexual orientation—more likely to abuse teenage boys than are heterosexual priests to abuse teenage girls. Here again, it is less the sexual orientation of the individual priest than predisposing factors apart from orientation that determine whether a man will offend against a minor.

Why then does it seem that priests who sexually abuse adolescents tend to abuse males? Part of the answer may be perception—these are the cases that receive the most publicity—and part of the answer may have to do with demographics.

Although reliable statistics are hard to come by, anecdotal reports suggest that there is a higher percentage of homosexually oriented individuals in the priesthood than in society generally. If so, then it is reasonable to expect that among those priests who abuse adolescents a higher proportion will be gay, not because gay individuals as such are predisposed to offend, but because there are more gay men in the priesthood. The inclination to abuse a minor proceeds from multiple factors and is only incidentally related to sexual orientation. It would be wrong to exclude a man from holy orders on the basis of sexual orientation alone in an attempt to stem the abuse of children and adolescents.

A Search for Understanding

In the course of my clinical practice, I have treated many individuals who were sexually abused as children and adolescents. Their circumstances differ, and the consequences of the abuse vary. The strength of their character and their willingness to carry on despite sometimes daunting odds testify to their resilience and to the grace of God. Yet though they differ, survivors of sexual abuse commonly pose two questions: "Why did this happen?" and "What can be done to prevent it in the future?"

The church would serve honorably by helping to answer these questions. To do so, it must withstand the current glare of media attention, act justly in a litigious climate and resist facile answers even from within its own ranks. It must also be willing to hear unwelcome truths and to act upon them rightly. If it does, then it can lend its enormous intellectual, pastoral and human resources to a concerted search for understanding and a remedy. In doing so, it will help to fulfill for survivors the vision of St. John in the Book of Revelation: "God himself will be with them; he will wipe away every tear from their eyes, and death shall be no more, neither shall there be mourning nor crying out nor pain any more, for the former things have passed away."

Periodical Bibliography

The following articles have been selected to supplement the diverse views presented in this chapter.

Vern L. Bullough — "Priests Are Human, and Sexual, Too," *Free Inquiry*, Winter 2000.

William Byron — "Thinking Systemically: Church in Crisis," *Origins*, May 16, 2002.

Mary Eberstadt — "The Elephant in the Sacristy," *Weekly Standard*, June 17, 2002.

Christopher Hitchens — "Pedophilia's Double Standard," *Free Inquiry*, Summer 2002.

Kenneth Jost — "Sexual Abuse and the Clergy," *CQ Researcher*, May 3, 2002.

John F. Kavanaugh — "Abusing the Truth," *America*, May 27, 2002.

Eugene Kennedy — "The Secret Cause of the Sex Abuse Scandal," *National Catholic Reporter*, June 11, 2002.

Bernard Law — "The Necessary Dimensions of a Sexual Abuse Policy," *Origins*, April 25, 2002.

John Leo — "Battle over Priests Could Result in Revolution," *Conservative Chronicle*, April 3, 2002.

Dan Michalski — "The Price of Priestly Pederasty," *Crisis*, October 2001.

Clarence Page — "Church Needs to Provide Moral Clarity," *Liberal Opinion Week*, May 6, 2002.

John R. Quinn — "Considerations for a Church in Crisis," *America*, May 27, 2002.

Charley Reese — "Child Abusers Deserve No Break," *Conservative Chronicle*, July 31, 2002.

Rosemary Radford Ruether — "Abuse a Consequence of Historic Wrong Turn: Priesthood and Celibacy Need to Be Distinct Vocations Once Again," *National Catholic Reporter*, June 7, 2002.

Carol Zaleski — "In Defense of Celibacy," *Christian Century*, May 8, 2002.

CHAPTER 3

How Should the Legal System Combat Child Sexual Exploitation?

Chapter Preface

Some think the sexual exploitation of children exists in some netherworld far from daily life, but research reveals that the sexual abuse of children is thriving on the Internet. A 2001 report prepared by the National Center for Missing & Exploited Children (NCMEC) revealed that children who use the Internet frequently report that they are exposed to unwanted sexual material, solicitation, and harassment. However, these children seldom report their experiences to their parents. The NCMEC claims that child sexual exploitation on the Internet is the most underreported crime in the United States. Law enforcement agencies suggest that because the Internet is easily accessible and relatively anonymous, online child sexual exploitation may be one of the most difficult crimes to combat.

Sexual predators who use the Internet are not dirty old men in trench coats lurking with bags of candy down at the school yard. They are often highly intelligent, outwardly normal young men willing to wait as long as it takes to gain a child's trust. FBI statistics reveal that the majority of Internet pedophiles are white males between the ages of twenty-five and forty-five. According to Special Agent Pete Gulotta of the FBI, "we've [arrested] military officers with high clearances, pediatricians, lawyers, school principals, and tech executives."

If these predators are difficult to spot in the community, they are even more difficult to recognize on the Internet. Sexual predators can assume any identity and troll through chat rooms looking for vulnerable children with little risk of being caught. Parents used to simply tell their children not to go out alone or talk to strangers, but today's parents need to understand technology to protect their children. Unfortunately, most parents are unaware that children view objectionable material and communicate with sexual predators. According to Donna Rice Hughes, author of *Kids Online*, "pedophiles and pornographers are exploiting technology for their advantage, and they are way ahead of parents." Law enforcement authorities agree: "The Internet has been a godsend to these people," says James McLaughlin, a detective in Keene, New Hampshire. McLaughlin's department found more than forty thousand pornographic images of children on one suspect's computer drive.

Some commentators dismiss the claim that Internet pedophiles pose as great a risk as political and media forces claim. Because the Internet is new technology, they argue, it evokes fear in those who are unfamiliar with it and becomes what the *Liberal Arts Mafia* calls "a new world bogeyman." These skeptics maintain that the media sensationalizes Internet pedophilia, affirming people's fears with stories of teenagers lured from chat rooms into liaisons with adults. Law enforcement reinforces these fears, claiming that technology makes these crimes almost impossible to track. Compared to other crimes against children, these commentators suggest, online pedophilia is relatively uncommon.

Whether the sexual abuse of children on the Internet is serious enough to require new laws and enhanced police powers is hotly debated. The viewpoints in the following chapter discuss these and other legal issues involved in efforts to address the sexual exploitation of children.

*"The universal adoption of sex offenders'
registration laws reflects the importance of
the interests they serve and the states'
belief in their efficacy."*

Community Notification Laws Protect Children from Child Molesters

Suzanne D. DiNubile

All states have enacted community notification laws that allow public access to information on sex offenders in the community, claims Suzanne D. DiNubile in the following viewpoint. Americans believe that these laws protect children, and protecting children outweighs the privacy and due process rights of child molesters, the author argues. According to DiNubile, the Supreme Court needs to uphold community notification laws and provide guidance so that states can write laws that withstand constitutional challenges. DiNubile is an attorney and director of business development for Medbiz, Inc., an online medical supplies and services company.

As you read, consider the following questions:
1. In DiNubile's opinion, how have states tailored successful sex offender registration and notification laws?
2. According to the author, what concerns do those opposed to Megan's Law have?
3. What does the author suggest sex offenders do if their shame is an obstacle in their life?

Suzanne D. DiNubile, "Supreme Court Reviews Predator Registration," *Klaas Action Review*, vol. 8, Spring 2002, p. 4. Copyright © 2002 by KlaasKids Foundation for Children. Reproduced by permission.

Public notification of sex offender release has been in place as a national law for almost a decade. In 1994, the Jacob Wetterling Crimes Against Children and Sexually Violent Offender Registration Act was enacted. This Act required all states to establish registration programs for sex offenders by September 1997. The law is designed to protect children and was named after Jacob Wetterling, an eleven-year-old boy who was kidnapped in October 1989. Megan's Law, the first amendment to the Jacob Wetterling Crimes Against Children and Sexually Violent Offenders Act, was passed in October 1996. Megan's Law mandated all states to develop notification protocols that allow public access to information about sex offenders in the community. Megan's Law was named after Megan Kanka, a seven-year-old girl who was raped and murdered by a twice-convicted child molester living in her New Jersey neighborhood.

However, these laws have not been easily accepted by our society, and continue to face challenge after challenge in court. Courts also often dissent from each other in determining the constitutionality of such laws. The Supreme Court is preparing to review these issues [during its October 2002 term].

Conflicting Decisions

On February 19, 2002, the U.S. Supreme Court announced that it will review the Ninth Circuit Court of Appeals decision which struck down the Alaska Sex Offender Registration Statute, on the grounds that it violated the Ex Post Facto Clause of the Constitution (which prevents a state from increasing the punishment for a crime after the crime is committed). States are able to place restrictions on a defendant after the crime is committed and time is served as long as they are not punitive. With Megan's Law, the Ex Post Facto issue is whether an offender whose offense was committed prior to the enactment of the statute should be subject to the statute.

The Ninth Circuit held that the Alaska statute is punitive and thus violates the Ex Post Facto Clause. However, the Tenth Circuit held that the Utah statute is not punitive.

The Tenth Circuit Court noted that Internet notification

represents merely a technological extension, not a sea change, in our nation's long history. It makes information public regarding criminal offenses, and the farther removed one is from a sex offender's community, the less likely one will be to have an interest in accessing the particular registry.

In contrast, the Ninth Circuit concluded that the Internet does not limit its dissemination to those to whom the particular offender may be of concern, so it is beyond that which is necessary to promote public safety. Also, by broadcasting the information about all past sex offenders, the Internet exposes all registrants to worldwide ostracism that damages them personally and professionally and could make it impossible for the offender to find housing or employment.

The End Justifies the Means

One factor considered in determining whether a law is punitive is if it has historically been used as means of punishment. The Tenth, Ninth, Sixth, Third, and Second Circuit Courts have rejected the pedophile's analogy to shaming practices in Colonial times, because those practices, unlike Megan's Law, inflicted physical punishment. The person was either physically held up before his fellow citizens for shaming, or physically removed from the community.

The Ninth Circuit stated that the law amounted to punishment, since offenders must re-register four times per year for the rest of their lives and cannot escape the Act's grasp, no matter how demonstrable it may be that they pose no future risk to anyone. The court noted that with the exception of the Tenth Circuit, every sex offender registration and notification law that has been upheld by a Federal Courts of Appeals has tailored the provisions of the statute to the risk posed by the offender.

However, the Tenth Circuit rejected this analysis, stating that although other states have chosen to incorporate more defined risk assessment mechanisms, a statute is not necessarily punitive because a state has not achieved a perfect fit between ends and means. Thus, the considerable assistance Internet notification will offer in the prevention, avoidance and investigation of these serious and damaging crimes justifies the means employed.

Examining Constitutional Challenges

The U.S. District Court for the District of New Jersey ruled on December 6, 2001, that the disclosure of convicted sex offenders' home addresses on the Internet violates their constitutional right to privacy. In finding that the registry violated the sex-offenders' privacy rights with respect to their home addresses, the court relied on the Paul P. cases, which examined similar law and concluded that "registrants possess a 'nontrivial' privacy interest in the confidentiality of their precise home address which is entitled to constitutional protection."

The court also held that the disclosure of the other information about sex offenders in the registry is not subject to a constitutional privacy right. The Court of Appeals for the Ninth Circuit had upheld Washington state's version of Megan's Law against a similar claim, in which plaintiffs failed to demonstrate the existence of a legitimate privacy interest in preventing the compilation and dissemination of truthful information that is already, albeit less conveniently, a matter of public record.

The Hawaii Supreme Court held in November 2001 that the Internet notification provisions of the Hawaii Statute violated the Due Process Clause of the Hawaii Constitution. This was because the statute did not allow for notice and a hearing in which the sex offender is given a meaningful opportunity to argue that he does not represent a threat to the community before disseminating the information on the Internet.

Preserving Megan's Law

Every state in the U.S. has now enacted a version of Megan's Law. The objective is to limit recidivism by alerting the public to potential threats to public safety posed by convicted sex offenders. The universal adoption of sex offenders' registration laws reflects the importance of the interests they serve and the states' belief in their efficacy. Approximately 30 states have already made registration and notification information available on the Internet. The Supreme Court should decide that the Alaska Statute does not violate the Ex Post Facto Clause. The Court should give guidance in its decision so that lower courts can identify any constitutionally problematic provisions and leave the rest of the states' registration and notification schemes in place.

The Tenth Circuit's decision is correct. Internet access to already available public information is merely an efficient way to organize and disseminate the important information needed to protect a community.

Those opposed to Megan's Law raise the concern of vigilantism. This is a minor issue compared to the violence that takes place against children when this information is not disseminated. Moreover, there is a caveat in bold type along with the information on each web site stating that the information should not be used to harass an offender and there are severe penalties for doing so.

The Registration Requirements

Although sex offender registration requirements vary according to state laws, some common features exist in registries across the country. In most states, the state criminal justice agency or board maintains the state's registry. Sex offenders register at local law enforcement or corrections agencies, which then forward the information to the state's central registry. Registry information typically includes the offender's name, address, date of birth, social security number, and physical description, as well as fingerprints and a photograph.

Alan D. Scholle, *FBI Law Enforcement Bulletin*, July 2000.

Any ostracism and scorn felt by a sex offender stems only from his own shame about the act or acts he has committed. As the Third Circuit stated, "the 'sting' results from the dissemination of accurate public record information about their past criminal activities." If this shame is such an obstacle in a sex offender's life, he should seek psychological counseling, as his victims must if they expect to lead a normal life. There is no obligation for the state to keep public information inaccessible just to prevent a sex offender from feeling victimized.

Insofar as employment is concerned, it is up to particular employers who they want to hire. If the choice is between a non-sex offender or a sex offender, employers are entitled to information to determine the best candidates. If the job involves working with children in any capacity, there is a tremendous state interest in having the information readily available.

The Power of the Internet

The Internet provides an opportunity for great advancement in the protection of the children of America. Technology has added greater efficiency to the notification scheme with very little cost. The Utah statute, for example, was motivated by a request to quickly check approximately 100,000 volunteers submitted by the Boy Scouts. In the fast-paced and nomadic communities we live in today, technology provides good citizens with a tool to help protect children. In addition, the registration and notification requirement scheme facilitates a widespread deterrent against sex crimes, since offenders presumably do not want the information disseminated.

Law enforcement must keep up with technology in order to stay ahead of the offenders. It has recently been reported that the Internet is to blame for a boom in child sex abuse. Information technology is exploding and if the "information superhighway" cannot be used to help stop crime and protect our children, but only can be used as a tool to facilitate crime, our children are in grave danger.

Opponents of Internet notification argue that it could foster a false sense of security. In other words, if a young family figures all the potential offenders in the community are listed on a web page, they may let their guard down around dangerous people not listed on the site, assuming they are safe. This only emphasizes the fact that we must educate and promote community awareness along with registration and notification.

In addition, there should be severe and uniform penalties for non-compliance. This way offenders will be diligent in registering and will not be inclined to retreat to a state that is softer on sex offenders.

"Public notification of sex offender release, Megan's Law, is one example of 'feel-good legislation' that has led to harmful conditions rather than the betterment or safety of society."

Community Notification Laws Are Unjust

Robert E. Freeman-Longo

In the following viewpoint, Robert E. Freeman-Longo claims that community notification laws, which allow public access to information on sex offenders in the community, are an emotional response to a serious problem, often causing more harm than good. Notification laws have been implemented, argues Freeman-Longo, despite the fact that no evidence proves that they reduce sex crimes against children. Moreover, numerous instances reveal that some of these poorly planned laws have hurt innocent victims, the author maintains. Freeman-Longo writes on sexual abuse prevention and is cofounder of the Association for the Treatment of Sexual Abusers and director of the Safer Society Foundation, Inc.

As you read, consider the following questions:
1. According to Freeman-Longo, why does the Internet increase problems with state sex offender registries?
2. What does the author believe may happen to communities' sense of safety as notification laws identify increasing numbers of sex offenders?
3. In the author's opinion, why is basing public notification on the dangerousness of the sex offender problematic?

Robert E. Freeman-Longo, "Revisiting Megan's Law and Sex Offender Registration: Prevention or Problem," *Sexual Violence: Policies, Practices, and Challenges in the United States and Canada*, edited by James F. Hodgson and Debra S. Kelley. Westport, CT: Praeger, 2002. Copyright © 2002 by James F. Hodgson and Debra S. Kelley. Reproduced by permission of Greenwood Publishing Group, Inc., Westport, CT.

Public notification of sex offender release has been in place as a national policy since 1996. In 1994, the Jacob Wetterling Crimes Against Children and Sexually Violent Offender Registration Act was enacted. The Jacob Wetterling Act required all states to establish stringent registration programs for sex offenders by September 1997, including the identification and registration of lifelong sexual predators. The Jacob Wetterling Act is a national law that is designed to protect children and was named after Jacob Wetterling, an eleven-year-old boy who was kidnapped in October 1989. Jacob is still missing. Megan's Law, the first amendment to the Jacob Wetterling Crimes Against Children and Sexually Violent Offenders Act, was passed in October 1996. Megan's Law mandated all states to develop notification protocols that allow public access to information about sex offenders in the community. Megan's Law was named after Megan Kanka, a seven-year-old girl who was raped and murdered by a twice convicted child molester in her New Jersey neighborhood.

Sensationalized cases, such as the rape and murder of seven-year-old Megan Kanka of Hamilton, New Jersey, have shocked and angered our society. The public is rightfully outraged at the nation's level of crime, particularly sexual crimes. Unfortunately, the public response is often more emotional than logical. During the 1990s, many legislative actions regarding sex offenders appeared to result from emotional public response to violent crime rather than from research showing that these laws will make any difference in correcting the problem and reducing crime. The laws sound and feel good when they are passed, but they may give citizens a false sense of security. Public notification of sex offender release, Megan's Law, is one example of "feel-good legislation" that has led to harmful conditions rather than the betterment or safety of society. . . .

The Problems with Megan's Law

Initially, public notification laws were proposed in response to the public's reactions to horrific crimes. Often, these crimes have been rape-murders, or extremely violent assaults on victims. Contrary to public belief, the vast majority of sexual offenses do not involve murder or violent assault of the victim. In fact, rape-murders and sadistic assaults account for less than 3 percent of all committed sex offenses. Unfortunately, Megan's Law and sex offender registration laws have been used even in cases involving incest and have resulted in families and victims being identified and harassed. In a January 2000 article, as a result of a class action suit, a federal judge has ordered New Jersey to rework its Megan's Law and threatened to shut down the notification process if prosecutors cannot put tighter controls on who receives information. Judge Joseph Irenas noted that New Jersey has failed to implement consistent standards of how notifications were conducted.

As of 2002, states with public notification laws had not yet offered scientific evidence to support the efficacy of such laws in promoting community protection and safety. Washington, which passed a public notification law in 1990, preceding Megan's Law, is the only state that has researched the efficacy of its public notification law. The State of Washington found no reduction in sex crimes against children: however, a benefit was the level of community education regarding sex crimes. As of 2002, there are no other published studies that demonstrate the efficacy of Megan's Law.

Public notification requires continuous monitoring by public service agencies (police, courts, and probation and parole agencies) to ensure offender compliance. All states have had to finance the costs of this mandated law (which did not come with funding for implementation). States face losing federal funding if they do not implement the law, but they do not have the resources necessary to implement it properly. Many states report that the registered addresses are not updated, and in many cases, incorrect addresses have been given. Many states post these on the Internet, listing innocent people's addresses as those of convicted sex offenders. Additional and unexpected costs also have been associated with these laws, further taxing social and criminal justice agencies. . . .

Public notification may lead to further violence. Some states already have experienced vigilante activities. The violence is not limited to convicted and registered/notified sex offenders. In many cases, innocent people, mistaken for sex offenders, have been assaulted or had their property damaged.

Among the most notorious cases of violence and vigilantism resulting from Megan's Law was the burning down of a sex offender's house in the State of Washington. Another that occurred in New Jersey involved the mistaken identity of a man who was thought to be a sex offender. His house was broken into, and he was severely beaten, resulting in the need for hospitalization.

A Simplistic Solution

No one wants a person likely to molest a child living next door. But legislators have tried to address a serious and complex problem, deviant sexual behavior, with an overly simplistic solution. Notification laws are an inadequate response to the problem of sexual offenses against children, which commonly are committed behind closed doors by a family member or friend.

Elizabeth Schroeder, *Los Angeles Times*, January 28, 1997.

The American Psychiatric Association's *Diagnostic and Statistical Manual of Mental Disorders-IV* classifies the sexual abuse of children under a diagnostic category known as pedophilia. Public notification laws require that this mental health/medical diagnosis be made public, whereas many other harmful conditions and behaviors remain private.

The use of confidentiality waivers is commonplace in working with sex offenders. Unfortunately, when the details of their lives and crimes are posted on public registries and divulged through notification, it is not only the offenders' confidentiality that is violated. Through the misuse and abuse of these laws, the names and addresses of families and, in some cases, the victims of sexual abuse are revealed.

Asking Constitutional Questions

The constitutionality of registration and public notification laws and an individual's right to privacy have undergone considerable debate. State registries on the Internet have increased the problem around these issues. It is no longer a community that knows about a specific offender, his address, and the particulars about his crime, but the entire world—anyone with access to the Internet—can have access to this information.

Federal laws regarding sex offender registries, public notification, and now those laws that address sexual predators and civil commitment also have been under legal scrutiny.

There have been, and continue to be, legal challenges to registration and notification laws in several states. However, predator laws are beginning to come under fire. On January 10, 2000, the Supreme Court "refused to revive Pennsylvania's law requiring that some sex offenders be designated as 'sexually violent predators' subject to lifetime registration and public notice of their address." The law was struck down and labeled as "constitutionally repugnant."

Legal scholars and others have looked at public notification as a form of punishment. There are several examples of how professionals and others have used this law beyond the way it was designed. For example, in some cases, law enforcement personnel have organized neighborhoods to exclude sex offenders from housing. In addition, law enforcement officers and others have released inaccurate information about registered sex offenders and/or those subject to notification laws. When these laws harm sex offenders and others, such as families and other community members, beyond the intent of the law, how can one not consider the impact as cruel, unusual, and excessive punishment? . . .

A False Sense of Security

Public notification is an easy solution to the highly emotional issue of sexual offending. The very nature of the law leads one to believe that by knowing where sex offenders live, one will feel safer. Safety is more than knowing. Some people feel more anxious knowing they now live near a convicted sex offender. Others cannot sell their homes when they want to move and known sex offenders are residing in nearby housing.

In St. Louis, Missouri, more than 700 registered sex offenders, or approximately 46 percent, do not live at the addresses posted on the sex offender registry, and many sex offenders (approximately 285 sex offenders released from prison as of May 1999) never get put on the list. With this and similar situations, can one truly feel more safe? Misinformation can be more damaging than no information.

As sex offender registration and public notification laws begin to identify an increasing number of offenders, these laws will create increasing levels of panic and possibly may begin to terrorize communities. One can only feel so safe knowing that there are sex offenders moving into and living in one's neighborhood and community. In some cases there are concentrations of sex offenders living in certain neighborhoods. As numbers increase and citizens become more concerned, more drastic measures to address the issue may result. . . .

The Impact on Victims

Public notification affects more than just offenders. When left to individual state discretion, many states have carried these laws to the extreme.

In Virginia, these laws have had an impact on victims and the families of convicted sex offenders. In one case, the wife and family (including the daughter who was also the victim) were harassed when the registry went on the Internet and their address was posted, even though the offender was sentenced to prison where he will remain incarcerated for some time. Despite the offender being in prison, his family's address was posted on the Internet as the address of a convicted sex offender.

The impact of public notification goes well beyond the offender and, in some cases, even beyond the victim. Highly publicized cases have demonstrated a severe and negative impact on the victim's family and the offender's family. In other instances, innocent persons, incorrectly identified as sex offenders, have been harassed and assaulted. . . .

Making Poor Decisions

Sexual offense cases are often weak in evidence, resulting in plea bargains to lesser offenses. With the coming of sex offender registration and community notification laws, persons charged with sex offenses now have a greater motive to avoid prosecution and to plea-bargain their crimes to lesser, nonsexual crimes. In some cases, social workers and child protection workers are reluctant to report cases involving juvenile sexual abusers to authorities out of concern that these young persons will be subjected to sex offender registration and community notification laws. In these cases many are quietly and privately referring these young persons to sex offender treatment specialists to get them treatment without the negative consequences of the law.

New Jersey and other states hate established levels of public notification based on a determination of the dangerousness of the particular offender in question. There is no consistent tool being used to determine risk, and in many states, risk is not determined by trained professionals or by the use of researched and reliable risk scales. In other cases, risk assessments are misused or misinterpreted to make individuals look more dangerous than they are. . . .

Responding to Serious Problems

Getting tough on crime, the death penalty, and "three strikes" sentencing options stem from emotional responses to serious societal problems and crime. Such "get tough laws on crime have not always proven to be effective and, in some cases, have made managing crime worse." Registration and public notification of sex offender release laws appear to be headed down a similar path. . . .

There is no doubt that unexpected problems and blatant abuses of sex offender registration and notification laws have occurred. Many of these were foreseeable and could have been avoided with more planning, research, and forethought about potential problems. I hope that we will not take another five or six years to revise these laws. The laws need to be more uniform between states, less punitive and destructive to sex offenders, less destructive to the lives of innocent persons, and more preventive (even though prevention will only occur in a limited way with these laws). Until we look at them closely and research their potential effectiveness, laws designed to protect our citizens may instead do more damage than if they did not exist at all.

VIEWPOINT

*"More can and should be done to keep
sexual predators from being able to reach
our children through the Internet and
commercial services."*

Expanding Police Powers Will Protect Children from Sexual Exploitation on the Internet

Louis J. Freeh

In the following excerpt from his testimony before a Senate Appropriations Subcommittee, Louis J. Freeh argues that government support of the FBI's "Innocent Images" program in which undercover agents pose as children or sexual predators has enabled law enforcement to successfully target online sexual predators. However, Freeh maintains, to effectively pursue those who exploit children on the Internet, law enforcement must be allowed to access encrypted communications and obtain Internet subscriber identities. Moreover, he claims, a nationwide database of DNA profiles and a national sex offender registry are necessary to quickly identify suspects. At the time of his testimony, Freeh was director of the Federal Bureau of Investigation. He retired in May 2001.

As you read, consider the following questions:

1. According to Freeh, on what particular sexual predator activities does the "Innocent Images" program focus?
2. What does the author suggest may happen as more and more agencies develop undercover child exploitation investigations?

Louis J. Freeh, statement for the record on Child Pornography on the Internet and the Sexual Exploitation of Children Before the Senate Appropriations Subcommittee for the Departments of Commerce, Justice, and State, the Judiciary, and Related Agencies, Washington, D.C., March 10, 1998.

The FBI initiated its "Innocent Images" investigation in 1995 as an outgrowth of the investigation into the disappearance of ten-year-old George Stanley Burdynski, Jr., in Prince George's County, Maryland. Investigation into the activities of two suspects determined that adults were routinely using computers to transmit images of minors showing frontal nudity or sexually explicit conduct, and to lure minors into illicit sexual activities.

Focusing on Sexual Predators

"Innocent Images" focuses on individuals who indicate a willingness to travel for the purposes of engaging in sexual activity with a child; individuals who produce and/or distribute child pornography through the Internet and on-line services; and, individuals who post illegal images onto the Internet and on-line services. The FBI has investigated more than 70 cases involving pedophiles traveling interstate to meet minors for the purposes of engaging in illicit sexual relationships.

FBI Agents and other federal, state, and local investigators participating on the "Innocent Images" task force go on-line in an undercover capacity, posing as either young children or as sexual predators, to identify those individuals who are victimizing children. The coordinated effort has generated significant results: since 1995, the "Innocent Images" investigation has generated 328 search warrants, 62 consent searches, 162 indictments, 69 informations, 161 arrests, and 184 convictions.

I am particularly pleased to report that since March of 1997, the number of search warrants executed increased 62 percent; the number of indictments obtained increased 50 percent; the number of arrests increased 57 percent; and the number of convictions increased 45 percent.

We have started on-line "Innocent Images" investigations in our Los Angeles field office. We are also considering the need for on-line "Innocent Images" efforts in other field offices based upon workload and the identification of specialized user populations involved in on-line child pornography and related sexual offenses. All of these efforts will be coordinated with and through our Baltimore Field Office.

The "Innocent Images" initiative has expanded its investigative scope to include investigations involving news groups, Internet Relay Chat (IRC) and fileservers (also known as fserves).

I would like to comment briefly on several challenges that face not only the FBI, but all of law enforcement, as we move ahead in our efforts to combat Internet and online child pornography and sexual exploitation.

The Challenges for Combating Child Exploitation

When I testified before the Subcommittee on the FBI's 1999 budget request, I outlined for the Subcommittee a number of challenges facing the FBI as it moves toward the 21st century. One of these challenges is the growing use of encryption by criminals to conceal their illegal activities. The "Innocent Images" initiative has uncovered sexual predators who use encryption in their communication with each other and in the storage of their child pornography computer files. This encryption is extremely difficult, and often impossible, to defeat.

It is essential that law enforcement agencies at all levels of government maintain the ability, through court order, to access encrypted communications and data relating to illegal activity.

The FBI has designated its Baltimore Field Office as the national coordinator for its "Innocent Images" initiative. Investigations of "Innocent Images" referrals conducted by other FBI Field Offices are coordinated through Baltimore.

Coordinating Efforts

Numerous other federal, state, and local law enforcement agencies are initiating online undercover child exploitation investigations, some as part of task forces and others on an individual agency basis. As more law enforcement agencies begin to use this investigative technique, the likelihood that one agency will begin investigating another agency's undercover operation will increase. This is an obvious waste of very finite resources. On-line child exploitation investigations often cross jurisdictional lines and, in some instances, even national boundaries. Investigations that begin in one area may branch off to involve locations throughout the country and have links to other ongoing investigations. These types of cases must be coordinated among the various law enforcement agencies having jurisdiction. I believe the FBI is in a position to provide valuable and effective leadership to spearhead this national effort.

The 1998 Justice Appropriations Act provides $2.4 million to the Office of Justice Programs for grants to establish state and local law enforcement cyber-squads. This subcommittee also instructed that these cyber-squads follow the investigative protocols developed by the Department of Justice in the "Innocent Images" investigation. The Office of Juvenile Justice and Delinquency Prevention, the Child Exploitation and Obscenity Section of the Criminal Division, the FBI, and the National Center for Missing and Exploited Children are working closely together to develop a plan for the formation of eight regional state and local task forces using these funds.

I would like to see our "Innocent Images" initiative serve as a national clearinghouse, with links to a network of regional task forces staffed by federal, state, and local investigators. Such a clearinghouse and network would enhance support for, and coordination of, on-line child exploitation investigations and facilitate the sharing of intelligence information gathered through undercover sessions and cases.

Identifying Sexual Predators

Sexual predators have predictable behavior traits. Clinical research studies have found that the average child molester will have more than 70 victims throughout his lifetime. DNA profiles are one law enforcement tool that can be effective in quickly identifying suspects.

The FBI continues to work with states to establish the Combined DNA Information System (CODIS) that will allow state and local crime laboratories to exchange and compare DNA profiles electronically, thereby linking serial violent crimes and to identify suspects by matching DNA evidence to offender profiles. CODIS is operational in 86 crime laboratories in 36 states and the District of Columbia.

Currently, 48 of 50 states and all territories and possessions have enacted laws allowing the collection of DNA samples from convicted sex offenders and others convicted of violent crimes. We are working with the two states that do not have laws and expect those states to enact appropriate laws this year. At this time, there is no comparable effort to collect and maintain DNA samples from individuals convicted federally for sex crimes and other violent offenses. As a result of the "Innocent Images" initiative and other cases, more and more individuals are being convicted in Federal Court for sex offenses involving minors.

The Target Age of Online Sexual Solicitation

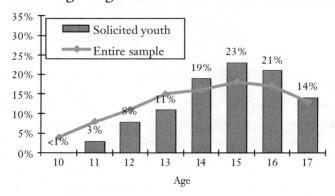

David Finkelhor, Kimberly J. Mitchell, and Janis Wolak, National Center for Missing & Exploited Children, 2002.

Steps need to be taken to close the gap between state and federal DNA profiling efforts so that a true nationwide database of DNA profiles for all convicted sex offenders is available.

The permanent national sex offender registry is scheduled to be implemented in July 1999 when the National Crime Information Center (NCIC) 2000 system becomes operational. This file will have the capability to retain an offender's current and previous registered addresses, dates of registration and conviction(s), photograph and fingerprints. Currently, an interim National Sex Offender Registry is operational which utilizes the FBI's Interstate Identification Index and the National Law Enforcement Telecommunications System. The initiative became operational in February 1997. As of February 12, 1998, 23 states are participating in the Registry with 30,778 records flagged as sex offenders.

Supporting Internet Industry Efforts

During 1997 and 1998, we have seen positive steps by the software and Internet Service Provider industries to reduce the availability of pornography to minors. Some Internet Service Providers are exploring different methods for protecting our children; to include blocking access to chat rooms and Internet news groups—the places where Sexual Predators target and recruit minors. Some site providers are using proof of age and similar shielding systems to keep underage children from accessing sites containing adult-oriented materials.

Yet, more can and should be done to keep sexual predators from being able to reach our children through the Internet and commercial services. I urge the manufacturers of software products, those used for connecting to the Internet and also used in modems and computers, to include with their products a copy of the Internet safety publications prepared by either the FBI, the National Center for Missing and Exploited Children, the Department of Education or a pamphlet of their own design. This simple action would help raise the awareness of parents and provide children with safety tips and practices to use while enjoying the Internet.

Accessing Subscriber Names

Another problem we encounter is access to subscriber information. When we identify an individual's screen name—not their subscriber name—through an on-line session, we must secure a Federal Grand Jury subpoena and then go to the Internet Service Provider to obtain subscriber and account information for that particular screen name. Oftentimes, sexual predators and others use multiple screen names or change screen names on a daily basis. Some Internet Service Providers retain screen name identifiers for such short periods of time—in some instances less than two days—that when law enforcement presents a subpoena, the Internet Service Provider is not able to retrieve from its archives the requested subscriber and account information.

The telephone industry is required by Federal Communications Commission regulation to maintain subscriber and call information for a fixed period of time. It would be beneficial for law enforcement if Internet Service Providers adopt a similar approach for retaining subscriber information and records for screen names and associated Internet Working Protocol numbers, or "IP addresses." Such information, when provided to law enforcement upon service of a subpoena, is critical to the timely identification of persons sending child pornography or trying to recruit a child for illicit sexual purposes.

Where possible, it would be beneficial for Internet service providers to capture and retain Caller ID data on persons accessing ISP lines. The capturing of Caller ID data will greatly assist law enforcement in child pornography/child sexual exploitation investigations.

Responding to Crimes Against Children

Our efforts to combat child pornography on the Internet and commercial service providers is one element of the FBI's comprehensive Crimes Against Children Initiative. The FBI's overall goal for its Crimes Against Children initiative is to provide a quick and effective response to all reported incidents. Through a timely response, we believe the FBI can, in conjunction with its law enforcement partners, increase the number of incidents in which the victimization of children is stopped and increase the likelihood that abducted or missing children are safely recovered.

In each of our field offices, we are reaching out to our state and local law enforcement partners to encourage them to notify the FBI within that critical first hour of a reported child abduction or missing child. Once notified, our goal is to rapidly deploy those resources necessary to support or conduct an investigation. . . .

No single law enforcement agency is equipped to handle the broad spectrum of issues that accompanies crimes against children. Working together, we can leverage our individual capabilities and expertise into an effective and comprehensive resource team. I have instructed each FBI field office to begin establishing multi-agency, multi-disciplinary resource teams consisting of federal, state and local law enforcement, prosecutors, victim/witness specialists, and health and social service professionals. These resource teams will facilitate interagency sharing of intelligence and information and enable effective investigation and prosecution of cases that transcend jurisdictional and geographical boundaries. . . .

I believe [Congress's] approach of balancing targeted increases in FBI investigative resources and capabilities in select areas with an emphasis on training for state and local law enforcement encourages partnerships and cooperation that are the keys to an effective response to the problem of Internet and on-line child pornography and child exploitation by sexual offenders and pedophiles.

"Recognizing a serious problem is one thing: using it as an excuse to implement dangerously bad laws is quite another."

Expanding Police Powers Is Unnecessary to Combat Child Sexual Exploitation on the Internet

Philip Jenkins

No evidence shows that enhanced police power will reduce the sexual exploitation of children through child pornography on the Internet, Philip Jenkins asserts in the following viewpoint. In fact, he maintains, enhancing police surveillance powers and restricting the use of encryption programs erodes personal liberties. Laws that combat the few who exploit children on the Internet, argues Jenkins, should not destroy the rights of the many who do not. Jenkins is a professor of history and religious studies at Pennsylvania State University and author of *Beyond Tolerance: Child Pornography on the Internet*, from which the following viewpoint was taken.

As you read, consider the following questions:
1. What does Jenkins say a person is revealing when he or she uses the Internet?
2. In the author's opinion, who are the courts encouraged to favor in cases involving threats to the young?
3. According to the author, what is flawed about law enforcement's argument against encryption?

Child pornography is a substantial presence on the Internet, and its potential audience is likely to grow rapidly as Internet usage expands. Given this fact, what, if anything, can be done? Is it possible to suggest solutions or responses that would not sabotage many of the positive aspects of the Internet? In other words, is there a cure that is not worse than the disease? Trafficking in Internet child porn may be so securely protected that total eradication could be achieved only by means that could not fail to damage many innocent users. Deciding which means are too severe or intrusive to combat this problem produces some troubling ethical debates. Briefly, do civil liberties and privacy rights end when one accesses the Internet? Some citizens may well place such a high value on child protection that they would accede to granting police or government the right to observe all Web traffic, to read all mail at random. Most of us, however, would be appalled by such an idea. So what is the proper balance between given technologies being both effective and tolerable?

Finding a Balance

This is not a simple transaction, a straightforward equation of "how many rights are you prepared to give up to safeguard children?" Repressive new laws theoretically directed against child porn might well cause injustice and inconvenience without having the slightest impact on that traffic. Recognizing a serious problem is one thing: using it as an excuse to implement dangerously bad laws is quite another. The answer to child porn is not to be found by adding ever more legal weapons to an already bulging police arsenal but rather in the proper deployment of existing powers and technologies.

From the outset, we have to realize what goals are achievable, and the total elimination of electronic child porn simply may not be within the bounds of possibility. That does not mean that we have to learn to accept or live with the problem, and we might well achieve a massive reduction of production and availability, on the lines of what was accomplished in the 1980s. The great majority of child porn users are rational enough to be deterred, if the proper methods are applied. If we could achieve, say, a 90 or 95 percent reduction of availability, that would be a massive victory in its own right. The fact that some residual trade will continue indefinitely should not provide grounds for ever-increasing encroachments on the liberties of law-abiding Netizens. . . .

The Erosion of Privacy on the Internet

If the traffic cannot altogether be eliminated, the next question is how far it can be detected and combated, with a view to suppressing the bulk of the trade and ending the present easy availability of this material. And how far can this be achieved without destroying the privacy rights of law-abiding Net users? When considering this, it is useful to recall just how far the Net has already eroded privacy, and the resentment that such intrusions have already caused. In reaction to current threats, legislators have come under pressure to enact safeguards from electronic snooping, at exactly the same time that the perceived need to combat cybercrime encourages the same lawmakers to enhance official surveillance powers. The result is a strange and fast-moving struggle of priorities, between what might be the irreconcilable values of individual privacy and public security.

One obvious privacy danger emerges from the linking of databases, permitting agencies or individuals, with or without authorization, to gather an astonishingly rich picture of the intimate lives of ordinary citizens. Personal, financial, and medical records thus become available to virtually anyone with a desire to investigate them. In Canada, for instance, virtually everyone who has ever had contact with an official agency has unwittingly volunteered to become the subject of an exceedingly detailed secret file, the like of which would have been beyond the wildest dreams of most traditional police states. . . .

Restricting Access

The obvious response, whether in Canada or elsewhere, is to place severe restrictions on access to such information, confining it to authorized agencies working under court warrants, which (unlike too much current practice) would be granted only in the rarest and most pressing of circumstances. Yet, as we will see, the demand to combat child porn and other cybercrime tends to expand rather than shrink the

Ignoring More Pressing Problems

Children have real problems in our culture, problems less spectacular but just as crippling as any Internet abduction. We need always to have them in mind, the children who are beaten, ignored, neglected and shut out, denied decent education, hope and love. We must answer to them as well, and right now our loud protestations of virtue, our declarations of willingness to protect, must ring hollow.

Who is being served by our willingness to rush headlong after problems, even before we know the problems exist? All it takes to get our undivided attention, it seems, is a problem that is spectacular, sexualized and far from home.

James R. Kincaid, *Salon*, August 24, 2002.

---

circumstances under which agencies can gain expedited access to information, often without troubling with the formalities of a judicial hearing.

Apart from official databases, anyone who uses the Internet, anywhere in the world, is likely to be assembling for him/herself a still more thorough dossier, revealing aspects of individual taste and preference, political, economic, literary, musical, and sexual. Some of the methods used are quite well known, such as the cookies [data stored on a personal computer that websites use to identify users who have visited the site] sent by a site to the computer that accesses it, which can be recognized by that or other servers. The implications are bothersome, to say the least. To take a simple example cited by journalist Mark Boal, imagine that the cookie evidence records that you visited *Koop.com* for cancer information and then went to the site of your insurance company. Does the linkage send up a red flag that leads the company to cancel your insurance? In a recent Texas lawsuit, a plaintiff protested that cookies violated the state's law against stalking and trespass. Clearly, this practice was not what legislators had in mind when they passed anti-stalking laws, but on reflection, what cookies do may well violate the letter of a law designed to protect individual privacy against persistent snooping. . . .

Combating Cybercrime, Destroying Liberty

Yet one clear political trend seems to be flatly contradicted by another, namely, the urge to combat cybercrime, a collection of concerns among which child pornography is prominently represented. As judges and legislators seek to defeat child porn, they are often enhancing the very threats to privacy and individual rights that, rhetorically, they are pledged to curb. In the process, tactics that might legitimately be applied against child pornographers (or spies, druglords, or terrorists) come to be applied to the vast majority of ordinary, law-abiding citizens. To put this in context, the attempt to suppress the misdeeds of (at a maximum) a hundred thousand people in the child porn subculture becomes the means of destroying the liberties of several hundred million others. This is a classic illustration of the adage that "hard cases make bad law."

As an ultimate evil, child porn has already justified various enhancements of law enforcement powers. Nations such as Britain historically have had a low regard for individual rights in the face of police powers, but disturbing legal precedents have also arisen in the United States. For example, most American states have laws against wiretapping, strictly regulating the circumstances in which authorities can gain access to private communications; but do such laws apply to accessing e-mail? This question often arises in cases involving threats to the young, and the need to protect the innocent encourages courts to find for the authorities. In a Pennsylvania cyberstalking prosecution, a judge determined that the state's wiretap law did not apply to the Internet. One wonders if judicial logic might have operated differently had the case at issue been less emotive, if sexual threats to children were not involved. A similar dynamic can be observed at the federal level. Armed with powers granted by the federal Sexual Predator Act of 1998, the FBI hopes to gain quicker access to online pornographers and pedophiles by subpoenaing online accounts directly, without court orders or grand-jury subpoenas.

An Excuse to Expand Police Power

Repeatedly, we find child porn and other sensational crimes used to justify expanding police powers over the electronic world, though it is difficult to see just what effect these measures have had, or could have, on the subculture itself. Encryption is an obvious example. During the 1990s, police agencies have expressed alarm at the spread of technologies that permit private citizens to send messages impervious to decoding by any outside party. The virtues of such encryption are obvious, as are the countless lawful circumstances in which people might wish to avoid prying eyes. A convincing case can also be made that the source code involved in encryption represents a form of constitutionally protected speech, in that it conveys a meaningful message much as musical notation does. Yet the spread of effective encryption has been delayed by the protests of law enforcement, particularly the FBI, who cite the dangers from terrorism, espionage, and child pornography. . . .

Preventing the Spread of Encryption

In consequence, the United States has fought a long war to prevent the spread of various encryption programs, to the extent that posting them on the Internet has prompted charges of exporting sensitive military technology. In 1993, the FBI and other federal agencies were demanding that so-called clipper chips be installed in all computers and other forms of electronic communication, in order to give federal agencies the capacity to exercise surveillance. In effect, this would have required all users of encryption to hand over the keys to the government, and the proposal was withdrawn after widespread protests. Nevertheless, similar efforts ensued, notably in attempts to dumb down telecommunications technology in order to permit wiretapping or to create "surveillance-friendly" e-mail systems. Since police agencies rarely possess the best or most advanced electronic technology, such proposals perforce open private communications to surveillance by many other unauthorized groups and individuals. The FBI has been clamoring for a proposed Cyberspace Electronic Security Act to give police access to codes to unscramble encrypted communications.

Law enforcement has similarly fought against other techniques intended to avoid electronic surveillance, whether by government or marketers. According to Mark Boal, one example of such a technique is the "Freedom" technology, which is designed to evade cookies by providing users with various fake identities, or "nyms": "Activate a nym before browsing, and cookies will be contained in that nym's own Cookie Jar. Even the smartest cookie can only reference the browsing history of the nym itself. . . . The specter of these foolproof fake IDs is precisely what interests our three-letter spy agencies. If such software were widely used, the Internet would change from a place where everybody leaves a data trail to one where newbies, pedophiles, and terrorists are equally cloaked." The development of "Freedom" has been possible only because the company involved is based in Canada. It is a telling commentary on the effects of police-inspired restrictions that much of the development of encryption has had to take place off American soil. Equally troubling is the underlying message that individuals should not be able to shield themselves against corporate exploitation because they would be using a technology that might, conceivably, be used by criminals.

As a rhetorical tactic, the argument made by the FBI and other "spy agencies" is superb, as it suggests that those who oppose restrictions on encryption must be, innocently or otherwise, favoring the interests of spies, terrorists, and child porn merchants. On closer examination, though, the arguments made by law enforcement have obvious flaws. Just to take the area of child porn, has there ever been a single investigation or prosecution that was stymied by lack of adequate legal powers or thwarted by encryption? When? Where? I have never heard of one and feel sure that the FBI would have trumpeted any such instance as part of its war against effective public access to encryption. Just to cite Freeh's example, if the images sent by the suspect could not be decrypted, how does the FBI know they constituted child porn? Did the agency decipher them in the end? Or, more likely, did they have so much other evidence to justify prosecution in this case that it mattered not a whit that a few suspect images remained unavailable?

Using Existing Resources

Apart from their intrinsic dangers, enhanced police powers are largely irrelevant to the fundamental child porn problem. As we have seen repeatedly, the failure to suppress child porn has not resulted from a shortage of such powers, nor from a shortage of adequate technology, since even with existing resources, significant victories have been achieved. There have been mass raids and arrests, some of which have broken up major child porn rings, and operations have demonstrated an impressive degree of international coordination. As one pedo [pedophilia] board participant writes, with not too much exaggeration:

> I think the US-Gov would do anything to get us. . . . LEA [Law Enforcement Agency] has strict rules there, but when US-Gov considers us the enemy, bending and breaking the rules may be an everyday thing. . . . The US has laws that loop and bend-over-backwards, all in the name of justice . . . you'd be surprised at what they would do to get anyone, anywhere, without creating too much attention.

Since 1999, server administrators, too, have cooperated much more closely with authorities to prevent the proliferation of temporary CP Web sites, and some once-preferred sites such as *angelfire* and *sexhound* are now off limits. Presumably, other servers will react more quickly if they find themselves being used by child porn merchants. Once they are aware of the danger, improving technology should make it much easier and quicker for search robots to identify and remove child porn postings. Many ISPs have shown themselves willing to report and suppress any child porn activity that comes to their attention. Most telling, hackers and private enterprise anti-pedophile groups have emerged as a serious challenge to the subculture, in a way that may well shift the balance in the ongoing struggle to the side of the authorities. No number of new laws or new police powers, no new restrictions on encryption, would fundamentally change this situation.

> *"Molesters excited by child porn who attack children don't give a damn whether it is real or virtual when the one is indistinguishable from the other."*

Computer-Generated Child Pornography Should Be Banned

Paul M. Rodriguez

Child pornography, whether real or computer-generated, encourages child molesters, argues Paul M. Rodriguez in the following viewpoint. The purpose of laws banning child pornography, he maintains, is to protect children from exploitation for its production and prevent child molesters from obtaining images known to whet their predatory appetites. Since computer-generated images of imaginary children engaging in virtual sexual acts are indistinguishable from real images, claims Rodriguez, they should be considered child pornography and banned. Paul M. Rodriguez is managing editor of *Insight* magazine.

As you read, consider the following questions:
1. According to Rodriguez, what are the laws against child pornography designed to accomplish?
2. What does the author suggest is part of the perversion that drives some to harm children?
3. In Rodriguez's opinion, what essential ingredient of the law against computer-generated child pornography did the Supreme Court dismiss?

Researching our story about the April 16, 2002, Supreme Court decision approving "virtual" child pornography, we wanted to present a visual image that would bring home the horror of this outrage. After extensive calls to the top photo sources failed to produce anything that approximated actual photography of the kind still banned by law, we turned to the Internet. Brother, what a shock it was to see what's out there on the World Wide Web. And we don't mean just every imaginable (or unimaginable) version of hard-core porn, but even the innocent listings that often are attached to pornographic materials.

Equally disturbing (and we'll explain this further on) were porn links that led through images and virtual graphics that seemed not to be pornography at all. In fact, a number of such "binary" sites we found with the help of savvy Webmasters were shocking because they began with the kind of harmless photographs and images of children that might be found in school yearbooks, family albums or Sunday-school bulletins.

The importance of the apparently innocent pictures is, in fact, at the core of our laws against child porn, and it eviscerates the Supreme Court's extraordinarily stupid decision that says virtual images of children used as sexual props is okay because no crime against real children is involved and so publication is protected by the First Amendment.

Examining Laws Against Child Porn

Pornography involving consenting adults invokes far different issues than child porn. Our society long ago distinguished the dramatic differences between the two and decided that the latter is aberrant, deviant, depraved and immoral. It endangers the safety of innocent children, which is why it is illegal. It harms children who are exploited foully to make it and it provides a potential catalyst for pederasts and other sexual perverts who may go from images to the real thing—a crime in which victims often are psychologically crippled or even murdered to ensure their silence. Society simply decided that the risk of child rape being excited by this stuff is too great to be tolerated.

Indeed, laws against child pornography are designed to

accomplish two things: 1) protect children from exploitation for its production and 2) create fire walls to prevent such material from being obtained by wanna-be, in-waiting or impulse-driven child-sex predators who the courts, law enforcement, victims and even the criminals themselves claim are excited to act out their loathsome fantasies by pornographic images of children. The medical profession long has believed that those convicted of child-sex abuse are unlikely ever to be cured of their "illness." Some penologists claim there literally is a 100 percent recidivism rate for pederasts.

Dix. © 1985 by *The Union Leader*. Reprinted with permission.

Which brings us back to those seemingly innocent photographs and images of children on the Internet. It puzzled us, so we followed an escalating trail of pornographic links with headers such as "virtual porn," "child porn" and similar variations. Not only were the pornographers baiting a virtual path to their hard-core sites with images of innocence, but whoever did this understood that their pederast clientele wants to pursue child sex by sorting through pictures of normal children. The search for the victim is part of the perversion that drives some to harm children.

Ignoring the Effects of Virtual Child Porn

Unless the government case was completely incompetent, the Supreme Court should have known all of this, yet it ignored the prevention aspects of the law against virtual child porn that it struck down. In doing this the court brazenly and irresponsibly dismissed an essential ingredient of that law: recognition of the effects even virtual child porn has on encouraging potential child molesters.

In conversations with some of the leading entrepreneurs of virtual technology we learned something else that the apparently ignorant Supreme Court majority overlooked. The industry already can create human images indistinguishable from images of real people and can animate them to do anything at all. Virtual reality is just that—images of computer-generated humans made to act in any way their creators wish them to behave. The same thing is being done pornographically, we're told, with virtual children engaging in sexual acts—children indistinguishable from real children to the pederasts, whetting their appetites for molestation.

Indeed, we're told by medical and law-enforcement experts, molesters excited by child porn who attack children don't give a damn whether it is real or virtual when the one is indistinguishable from the other. Unfortunately, in its rush to judgment, the liberal majority that now dominates the Supreme Court failed to see the bigger picture. For that matter, it failed even to see the images of real and virtual child porn that are indistinguishable.

Congress and the George W. Bush administration are working to overcome the high court's blunder. Perhaps part of that effort ought to include a cyber-warfare agency that employs the military or intelligence technology now used to hunt down terrorists via the Internet. It should be a relatively simple matter to apply existing child-porn standards against the international child-porn terrorists and their client-agents who are waging a real war against our very real children. Our kids are the ones who are "virtual" targets of child-porn predators.

Thank God we have the First Amendment. It allows us to say directly that the damned-fool Supreme Court justices responsible for this abomination should be horsewhipped.

*"Laws against depictions of imaginary
children can only rely on imaginary
evidence of harm."*

Laws Against Computer-Generated Child Pornography Are Unnecessary and Unfair

Wendy Kaminer

In the following viewpoint, Wendy Kaminer claims that there is little or no evidence that computer-generated images of imaginary children having virtual sex encourage child molesters. Laws against computer-generated pornography, Kaminer argues, are based on the unsubstantiated presumption that computer-generated child pornography encourages child molesters to molest children. This presumption, however, is based on the subjective responses of child molesters, she asserts, and is too vague to meet the requirements of laws that limit free speech. Kaminer is a lawyer, social critic, and senior correspondent for *American Prospect*.

As you read, consider the following questions:

1. According to Kaminer, what did the Ninth Circuit observe in the *Free Speech Coalition v. Reno* case?
2. What does the author believe is wrong with the reasoning that there is no difference in the effect produced by real and virtual child pornography?
3. Why does the author think defending material that violated a ban on virtual child pornography would have been difficult?

It is possible, of course, that computer-simulated images of virtual children having virtual sex may encourage pedophiles to act on their impulses or assist them in seducing children. There is, however, little or no empirical evidence that these images have such dire effects. Congress criminalized virtual child porn anyway.

Examining the Law

The Child Pornography Prevention Act of 1996 (CPPA) prohibited computer images that "appear" to show actual children engaged in sex; it also banned advertising, promoting, or describing any sexually explicit images "in such a manner that conveys the impression" that actual children are depicted. Antiporn activists insisted that this ban on virtual porn was essential to protecting children and enforcing laws against actual child pornography, since prosecutors may not be able to distinguish the actual from the virtual variety. Free speech advocates charged that the CPPA allowed for the prosecution of thought crimes, by criminalizing nonobscene images of imaginary children engaged in imaginary sex. The Supreme Court agreed: On April 16, 2002, in *Ashcroft v. Free Speech Coalition*, it struck down the virtual porn provisions of the CPPA, in a 6 to 3 decision. The Court left intact parts of the law that banned using or manipulating images of actual children to produce pornography; but it found the ban on virtual porn clearly unconstitutional because it "proscribe(d) the visual depiction of an idea." Writing for the majority, Justice [Anthony M.] Kennedy eloquently pointed out the obvious: "The right to think is the beginning of freedom, and speech must be protected from the government because speech is the beginning of thought."

Speech is the beginning of action, defenders of the virtual porn ban would respond, but as the Supreme Court has repeatedly held, the possible or presumed effects of speech do not justify its suppression. Criminal law is supposed to address the action, not the word—the act of child abuse, not the idea of it. Civil libertarians have long accepted (and supported) bans on depicting actual children engaged in actual sex. Traditional child porn laws need not rely on speculation about the harm caused by the distribution of sexually explicit images involving minors; they can rely instead on the harm caused by the *production* of sexually explicit images involving minors.

The Threat of Imaginary Harm

But laws against depictions of imaginary children can only rely on imaginary evidence of harm. As the Ninth Circuit observed in *Free Speech Coalition v. Reno*, in 1999: "Factual studies that establish the link between computer-generated child pornography and the subsequent sexual abuse of children apparently do not yet exist." Indeed, in enacting the CPPA, Congress invoked the report of the pornography commission led by former attorney general Meese in the 1980s, which only addressed the suspected harms of pornography involving actual children. In other words, the Ninth Circuit stressed, the CPPA relied on findings that "predate" the technology it targets.

Still, defenders of the CPPA equate actual and virtual porn, simply because they are difficult to distinguish visually. "Both actual and counterfeit child pornography will pass for the real thing and incite pedophiles to molest and children to be victims," according to the amicus brief filed by the National Law Center for Children and Families (and several other conservative advocacy groups). "If the pedophile and the child victim cannot tell the difference, there is no difference in the effect conveyed." What's wrong with this reasoning? (Put aside the callous disregard of the difference to real children who are forced to have sex in the production of real pornography.) It assumes its conclusion—that virtual child porn incites pedophilia and creates "child victims." It advocates criminalizing speech because of its presumed effect on a particular class of listeners—people inclined toward child abuse.

Courts have confronted this argument repeatedly in First Amendment cases, particularly in cases involving pornography. In 1985, in *American Booksellers Association v. Hudnut*, the Seventh Circuit Court of Appeals struck down a local antiporn ordinance based on the assumption that pornography leads to the objectification of women, contributing to sexual violence and discrimination. Accepting this assumption for the sake of argument, the court pointed out its inadequacies: "All of these unhappy effects depend on mental intermediation." In other words, the listener as well as the speaker determines the meaning and impact of any verbal or visual communication. That's why its consequences are unpredictable. The power of speech is collaborative.

A Subjective Determination

A ban on virtual child porn relies heavily on the subjective reactions of viewers, which means that speakers are given little notice of precisely what speech is criminalized. When Congress bans sexually explicit material that "appears" to depict minors engaged in sex, you have to ask "appears to whom?" A lot of people over forty have trouble distinguishing nineteen-year-olds from precocious fifteen-year-olds. The CPPA could easily have been construed to prohibit nonobscene sexually explicit images of young adults. Congress did provide targets of the law with a defense: that the alleged child porn involved an actual person, who was an adult at the time the image was produced (so this defense would not apply in cases of virtual child porn) *and* that the image was not promoted in a way that "conveyed the impression" that it involved a minor. "Conveyed to whom?" you have to ask.

What are people talking about when they talk about child

The Supreme Court Decides Virtual Child Porn Law Is Unconstitutional

The Government submits that virtual child pornography whets the appetites of pedophiles and encourages them to engage in illegal conduct. This rationale cannot sustain the provision in question [Child Pornography Prevention Act of 1996]. The mere tendency of speech to encourage unlawful acts is not a sufficient reason for banning it. The government "cannot constitutionally premise legislation on the desirability of controlling a person's private thoughts." First Amendment freedoms are most in danger when the government seeks to control thought or to justify its laws for that impermissible end. The right to think is the beginning of freedom, and speech must be protected from the government because speech is the beginning of thought.

Anthony M. Kennedy, *Ashcroft v. Free Speech Coalition*, April 16, 2002.

---

pornography? That depends. Some point to Calvin Klein ads or the movie version of *Lolita* [in which a forty-year-old man has a sexual relationship with a twelve-year-old girl], not to mention the book. Supreme Court Justice [Antonin] Scalia (who voted to uphold the CPPA) inadvertently confirmed the continuing vulnerability of *Lolita* during oral argument in *Ashcroft v. Free Speech Coalition*. When the attorney challenging the virtual porn ban offered "the movie *Lolita*" as an example of a work of art that the ban would imperil, Justice Scalia responded sarcastically, "A great work of art," adding "with all due respect" that *Lolita* "is not the *Mona Lisa* or the *Venus de Milo*." He's right that *Lolita* does not enjoy the universal acclaim of established Renaissance masterpieces, but his observation was irrelevant: Books, films, paintings, and other forms of speech need not occupy places in the pantheon of great art (or popular culture) in order to enjoy First Amendment protection. The First Amendment is not designed to protect either the *Venus de Milo* or Mickey Mouse. It's designed for the protection of contested, controversial works, like *Lolita*, or *Huckleberry Finn*. In Oklahoma City, *The Tin Drum*, the 1979 film based on the novel by Günter Grass, has been condemned as pornographic; in 1997, local officials confiscated copies of this allegedly dangerous film, which includes a scene suggestive of oral sex between a six-year-old boy and a teenage girl. A court in Oklahoma judged the film obscene.

A History of Censorship

People intent on restricting sexual imagery will dismiss cases like this as "horror stories," suggesting that they're rare or even apocryphal. In fact, they're fairly common, as anyone familiar with the recent history of censorship knows. In public schools and libraries across the country, censors intent on suppressing sexual explicitness or mere discussions of sexuality regularly target an odd assortment of books by such authors as Henry Miller, D.H. Lawrence, James Joyce, E.M. Forster, May Sarton, and Judy Blume.

These authors have impassioned defenders, of course, and they sometimes succeed in resisting censors who target works with acknowledged social or artistic value. (As a general rule, speech must be found to have no redeeming value to be considered obscene.) Defending material that allegedly violated a ban on virtual child porn would have been much more difficult, since evidence of social, scientific, or artistic value is irrelevant to a charge of child pornography.

The CPPA's bans on virtual child porn and suggestive advertising were doomed partly because they could easily have been applied to respected works of art (like *Romeo and Juliet*, the Supreme Court observed). But the broad reach of the law was not accidental. Retiring North Carolina senator Jesse Helms included some sex education materials in his definition of child porn. Not that attacks on sexually explicit or suggestive speech emanate only from the right. The CPPA was enacted with the support of centrist democrats, including Bill Clinton, who signed it into law. Sex does have inevitable perils (as the former president found out), but, thanks to the Supreme Court, fantasizing about sexual activity is, once again, not as risky as engaging in it.

Periodical Bibliography

The following articles have been selected to supplement the diverse views presented in this chapter.

Ernest E. Allen	"Virtual Child Pornography: The Impact of the Supreme Court Decision in the Case of *Ashcroft v. Free Speech Coalition*," testimony before U.S. House of Representatives Judiciary Committee Subcommittee on Crime, May 1, 2002. www.missingkids.com.
Daniel Armagh	"A Safety Net for the Internet: Protecting Our Children," *Juvenile Justice Journal*, May 1998.
Austin Bunn	"Digitizing Megan's Law," *Village Voice*, April 21, 1998.
John deLaubenfels	"Virtual Child Pornography," *Strike the Root.com*, July 31, 2002. www.strike-the-root.com.
Catherine Edwards	"Pedophiles Prowl the Internet," *Insight*, February 28, 2000.
Eric Felten	"'The Deal with Older Guys': There's Good Reason Americans Support Parental Notification Laws," *Weekly Standard*, August 19, 2002.
Jean Hellwege	"Law Enforcement, Legislators Grapple with Child Sexual Exploitation on the Net," *Trial*, March 2000.
Marc Klaas	"Community Notification: Does It Violate Human Rights?" *Klaas Action Review*, Fall 1998.
Liberal Arts Mafia	"The Fear of Pedophilia in a Brave New World," May 8, 2001. www.liberalartsmafia. com.
Alissa Quart	"Something Wicked This Way Comes," *Time*, June 5, 2000.
Maria Seminerio	"Pedophile Profile: Young, White, Wealthy," *ZDNet News*, September 19, 1999.
Chitaporn Vanaspong	"Dangerous Chat: Stopping the Spread of Child Pornography on the Internet," *Toward Freedom*, Winter 1998/99.
William Woodward	"Beyond Megan's Law," *State Government News*, May 2001.
Mary Sykes Wylie	"Secret Lives: Pedophilia and the Possibility of Forgiveness," *Networker*, November/December 1998.
Charmaine Yoest	"Not a Pretty Picture: The New Face of Kiddie Porn," *Women's Quarterly*, Spring 2000.

CHAPTER 4

How Can Child Abuse Be Reduced?

Chapter Preface

In 1999, on Super Bowl Sunday, two-year-old Miguel Arias-Baca lay dying on the bathroom floor of his Denver, Colorado, foster home. His foster father, upset that Miguel had soiled his diaper, smeared the boy's face in his own feces and threw him to the ground. Miguel's brain swelled with blood, but his foster parents waited more than four hours before they took him to the hospital. The child, covered in bruises, died.

As news of this tragic incident spread, people began to ask how such a thing could happen. After all, foster parents were supposed to be dedicated to caring for the children entrusted to their care. Indeed, foster care can provide a welcome refuge for children of abusive parents. However, critics of child protection programs argue that recent trends in child abuse policies promote foster care at the expense of the children they are designed to protect. As a result, they maintain, in many states not only has "for-profit" foster care become big business, but overburdened child protection agencies have difficulty monitoring the increasing number of children placed in foster care. Consequently, the abuse of foster children such as Miguel often goes unnoticed until it is too late.

While researching Miguel's case for the *Denver Post*, Patricia Callahan discovered the nature and scope of the foster care industry. She learned, for example, that taxpayer subsidies compensate foster care companies for placing and overseeing the care of abused and neglected children. According to the National Coalition for Child Protection Reform, these companies are paid for every day that they keep a child in foster care. If they return a child to his or her home, or make the child available for adoption, the reimbursement stops, creating a strong incentive to let children languish in foster care. In Colorado, Callahan writes, the number of foster homes recruited and supervised by private businesses had increased more than 800 percent between 1986 and 2000.

According to some analysts, in many states the rapidly expanding foster care industry has developed few mechanisms to oversee these companies. For example, Callahan claims that rather than personally insuring that foster care businesses were following state rules designed to protect children, overworked foster care officials in Colorado asked foster care companies to evaluate themselves by filling out a "self-assessment" form. "What business," Callahan asks, "was going to turn itself in for breaking state rules?"

Confidentiality statutes designed to protect the privacy of abused children also make it difficult to access information about foster parents. In order to access background information on foster parents, Callahan's investigative team created its own database and discovered that some of Colorado's foster care businesses either failed to investigate or ignored the fact that they recruited parents with criminal records, including Miguel's foster parents. Just about anyone, the team revealed, could become a foster parent in Colorado's foster care system: One woman recruited as a foster care mother had been charged with selling drugs out of her day care home; another recruited foster parent had spent half of his adult life in prison for robbery and assault.

Some observers suggest that welfare reform legislation—which forces parents off welfare after two years of assistance, making it more difficult for them to properly care for their children—has further contributed to a growth in the foster care industry. The organization Justice FOR Children reports that more than 50 percent of substantiated child abuse cases are due to neglect, which is often a result of poverty. These reform measures prevent impoverished parents from getting the public assistance they need to take care of their children. As a result of this "neglect," child protective services often remove the children from the home. As soon as these children are taken away and placed in foster care, the foster care system receives a never-ending subsidy to help foster parents cover child care costs. Unfortunately for the taxpayer, argues Justice FOR Children, the cost of foster care is much higher than the cost of welfare. A family of three, the organization reveals, would receive from $377 to $656 per month on welfare while a foster family would receive $1,350 to $5,400 per month.

To be sure, the foster care industry remains controversial. The authors in the following chapter offer their views on how the occurrence of child abuse—both within and outside the family—can be prevented.

> "*Intensive family preservation programs have a better record of safety than foster care.*"

Family Preservation Programs Are More Effective than Foster Care

National Coalition for Child Protection Reform

In the following viewpoint, the National Coalition for Child Protection Reform (NCCPR) claims that programs that attempt to keep abused children with their families keep children safer than programs that put them into foster care. For example, several studies reveal that child abuse fatalities are more likely to occur in foster care, the NCCPR maintains. In contrast, the NCCPR argues, programs that follow successful family preservation models have reduced child abuse and child abuse deaths. The NCCPR is an organization that opposes foster care and is committed to reforming the child protective system to make it less disruptive to families.

As you read, consider the following questions:
1. According to the NCCPR, why is the actual amount of abuse taking place in foster care likely to be higher than the maltreatment reported in studies?
2. What does the NCCPR say Alabama learned from other states?
3. What three reasons does NCCPR give for the success of family preservation programs?

At the heart of the criticism of family preservation is one overriding assumption: If you remove a child from the home, the child will be safe. If you leave a child at home the child is at risk. In fact, there is risk in either direction, but intensive family preservation programs have a better record of safety than foster care.

To understand why, one must first understand one fundamental fact about foster care: It's not safe. Here's how we know:

Examining Studies of Foster Care

National data on child abuse fatalities show that a child is more than twice as likely to die of abuse in foster care than in the general population.

A study of reported abuse in Baltimore found the rate of "substantiated" cases of sexual abuse in foster care more than four times higher than the rate in the general population. Using the same methodology, an Indiana study found three times more physical abuse and twice the rate of sexual abuse in foster homes than in the general population. In group homes there was more than ten times the rate of physical abuse and more than 28 times the rate of sexual abuse as in the general population, in part because so many children in the homes abused each other.

Those studies deal only with reported maltreatment. The actual amount of abuse in foster care is likely to be far higher, since agencies have a special incentive not to investigate such reports, since they are, in effect, investigating themselves. In New York City, for example, where Children's Rights Inc. settled a lawsuit against the child welfare system, [the original complaint against the city stated] that "Abuse or neglect by foster parents is not investigated because [agencies] tolerate behavior from foster parents which would be unacceptable by birth parents."

And a lawyer who represents children in Broward County, Florida, says in a sworn affidavit that over a period of just 18 months he was made personally aware of 50 instances of child-on-child sexual abuse involving more than 100 Broward County foster children. The official number during this same period: Seven—because until what the lawyer called "an epidemic of child-on-child sexual abuse" was exposed, the child abuse hotline didn't accept reports of such abuse.

Studies not limited to official reports produce even more alarming results. Another Baltimore study, this one examining case records, found abuse in 28 percent of the foster homes studied—more than one in four.

Even what is said to be a model foster care program, where caseloads are kept low and workers and foster parents get special training, is not immune. When alumni of the Casey Family Program were interviewed, 24 percent of the girls said they were victims of actual or attempted sexual abuse in their foster homes. Furthermore, this study asked only about abuse in the one foster home the children had been in the longest. A child who had been moved from a foster home precisely because she had been abused there after only a short stay would not even be counted. Officials at the program say they have since lowered the rate of all forms of abuse to "only" 12 percent, but this is based on an in-house survey of the program's own caseworkers, not outside interviews with the children themselves.

A Threat to the Family

Across the United States, thousands of families have been ripped apart by child "protection" bureaucracies. Parents in such circumstances find that if they have been "hot-lined"— that is, reported anonymously by a dutiful citizen, teacher, or acquaintance—they enjoy none of the rights and immunities associated with due process. Acting in the "best interests of the child," social workers can terminate parental rights on a whim, and order police agencies to enforce those whimsical decisions at gunpoint.

William Norman Grigg, *New American*, August 30, 1999.

This does not mean that all, or even many, foster parents are abusive. The overwhelming majority do the best they can for the children in their care—like the overwhelming majority of parents, period. But the abusive minority is large enough to cause serious concern. And abuse in foster care does not always mean abuse by foster parents. As happened so often during the Chicago Foster Care Panic for example, and as the Indiana study shows, it can be caused by foster children abusing each other.

Compare the record of foster care to the record of family preservation.

The original Homebuilders program [a Washington state program that provides intense, immediate involvement with families facing imminent removal of children to foster care] has served 12,000 families since 1982. No child has ever died during a Homebuilders intervention, and only one child has ever died afterwards, more than a decade ago.

Michigan has the nation's largest family preservation program. The program rigorously follows the Homebuilders model.

Since 1988, the Michigan family preservation program has served 90,000 children. During the first two years, two children died during the intervention. In the decade since, there has not been a single fatality. In contrast, when Illinois effectively abandoned family preservation, there were five child abuse deaths in foster care in just one year.

The other state in the forefront of family preservation efforts in recent years is Alabama. Alabama is implementing a consent decree *(R.C. v. Hornsby)* resulting from a federal lawsuit requiring it to reframe its whole approach to child welfare by following family preservation principles. Learning from the failures of other states which tried to change their systems overnight, the Alabama approach calls for gradual, county-by-county change. But the results already have been dramatic.

The number of children taken from their parents in 2001 was 20 percent lower than in 1997. And since 1996, re-abuse of children left in their own homes has been cut nearly in half. More important, an independent, court-appointed monitor concluded that children in Alabama are safer now than before the system switched to a family preservation model. The monitor wrote that "the data strongly support the conclusion that children and families are safer in counties that have implemented the R.C. reforms."

Why Family Preservation Works

There are three primary reasons for the better safety record of family preservation programs that follow the Homebuilders model.

- Most of the parents caught in the net of child protective services are not who most people think they are. [NCCPR refers to research showing that most are cases in which poverty has been confused with neglect.]
- When child welfare systems take family preservation seriously, foster care populations stabilize or decline. Workers have more time to find the children who really do need to be placed in foster care.
- Family preservation workers see families in many different settings for many hours at a time. Because of that, and because they are usually better trained than child protective workers, they are far more likely than conventional child protective workers to know when a family can't be preserved—and contrary to stereotype, they do place child safety first.

> *"Family preservation . . . is the benign name for a policy that can result in horrifying outcomes."*

Family Preservation Programs Put Children at Risk

Susan Orr

According to Susan Orr in the following viewpoint, family preservation programs return children to violent, abusive parents despite the fact that little evidence shows whether these programs actually rehabilitate parents and protect children. Family preservation programs, she argues, protect parents who would be jailed for committing the same violence against someone who was not their child. Moreover, Orr claims, abused children languish in foster care without the possibility of adoption while they wait for their parents to reform. Susan Orr is director of the Center for Social Policy at the Reason Public Policy Institute.

As you read, consider the following questions:

1. In Orr's opinion, what do advocates of family preservation believe is the reason parents harm their children?
2. What examples does the author provide illustrating the power that social service agencies have?
3. What, according to the author, helps faddish theories such as family preservation override common sense?

In July 1998, an appeals court judge rendered one of those verdicts that causes sane people to wonder what sort of delirium has taken hold of the justice system. Latrena Pixley, who'd been found guilty of murdering her six-week-old daughter in 1992, won a custody battle for her two-year-old son, Cornilous.

The little boy had been in the care of Pixley's parole officer, Laura Blankman, while Pixley—whose other two children remain in foster care—served her minimal sentence for the cold-blooded murder of her baby: three-to-five years' probation that required her to spend weekends in a halfway house. According to evidence presented during the murder trial, Pixley had smothered her infant daughter, Nakya, and disposed of the body in a dumpster before going out for the evening with her boyfriend.

A Surprising Verdict?

The judge, however, accepted her excuse that she was suffering from "post-partum depression" at the time of the killing, and let her off amazingly lightly (by contrast, when Pixley was found guilty of credit card fraud later that same year, she actually had to serve time in prison). She gave birth to Cornilous, her fourth child, in 1996, while still on probation. Because she could not keep him at the halfway house, Blankman offered to take him into her home at her own expense. Note this was a private offer: Social services did not see any pressing need to remove this new baby from his mother.

That's the wisdom a Maryland appellate court upheld. The judge ordered Blankman to return the boy to Pixley, despite the fact that Blankman wanted to keep caring for Cornilous and that she was the only mother he had ever known. For Cornilous, biology had become destiny.

Many were rightly staggered by the Pixley verdict: How could a judge award custody of a child to a convicted babykiller, whose other children remained in the care of others? But the Pixley case is, in fact, not surprising. It is the product of a policy known as "family preservation" that now governs child welfare agencies.

Family preservation, a form of therapeutic treatment that has been around since the 1970s, is the benign name for a policy that can result in horrifying outcomes. For what sensible person could be against preserving families? Its object is to stop parents who have already abused and neglected their children from doing so again. But it often turns into a perverse system of protecting the custody of parents who have records of hideously abusive behavior including, as in Pixley's case, child murder.

Advocates of family preservation believe that a parent harms a child because of undue pressure from stressful situations, such as being poor or uneducated. No parent willingly chooses to do evil: If a social worker could only intervene to ease and, if possible, remove the stress, the parent would do the right thing. Hence child welfare services allow case-workers to make themselves available, sometimes twenty-four hours a day, to a limited number of families for a short time (from six weeks to six months), in an attempt to get the family over a specific crisis and show the parents how to handle the stress without abusing or neglecting their children again.

In doing so, the worker will help organize every intimate detail of a family's life: teaching parenting skills; helping with the shopping, cleaning, and bill paying; providing transportation to appointments and counsel to family members. When intensive services are not provided, the theory surrounding family preservation still pervades day-to-day decisions about what to do with children in foster care: in short, keep them there for months, even years, until a parent has reformed. This utter faith in the benefits of therapy is what makes it possible for agencies to return a child to a mother like Latrena Pixley. As therapists assured the judge, Pixley was "over" the condition—post-partum depression— that caused her to kill her infant. She wasn't post-partum anymore—so why would she hurt little Cornilous?

The social workers' judgment, furthermore, is backed by enormous, and often arbitrary, state power, with the result that social service agencies now form among the most intrusive arms of government. Child welfare workers have the authority to intervene in domestic situations without a warrant, regardless of whether or not a crime has been committed. They have the power, in concert with cooperative courts, to separate parents from their children or, as it may be, to bring them back together. Child protective services can remove children from their homes when the agency determines a child is "at risk" of being harmed—but the definition of "at risk" is left largely up to the opinion of the social worker, upon whose judgment a judge heavily relies.

A Dangerous Policy

Half of the 1,500 children killed by their parents throughout the country each year are already known to the child welfare system. They are victims not of underfunding but of a more fundamental scandal: a "family preservation" policy that the federal government and 30 states, including New York, have carried to absurd and deadly extremes, putting children . . . at grave risk in the name of a skewed notion of civil liberties and parental rights.

Dennis Saffran, *City Journal*, Summer 1997.

The upshot is that while the details surrounding cases of child abuse and neglect are always gruesome, what is more grotesque is the fact that children often remain in danger long after they are known to authorities. Instead, case workers are giving truly awful, violent parents second, third, and fourth chances to do right by their children.

Unfortunately for Cornilous Pixley and others, there is scant evidence to support the family-preservationist belief that giving parents these chances, sprinkled with counseling sessions and case-worker intervention, actually works. Those who trumpet the success of family preservation will cite lower foster care rates as a result of it. But this is not true.

Questioning Family Preservation Policy

Of course, if one chooses not to remove children from dangerous homes, and instead "treat" them in-house, then the number of children in foster care declines automatically. Social scientist Peter Rossi, of the University of Massachusetts at Amherst, made himself unpopular in the world of child welfare experts by disputing the success of family preservation as being based upon flawed methodology. In his critical scholarly review of the policy, which was published in 1992 in *Children and Youth Services Review,* he cautioned evaluators to look at such factors as child safety and future rates of abuse as better measures of whether family preservation works. As well, Richard J. Gelles, director of the Family Violence Research Program at the University of Rhode Island, has observed that all rigorous studies of family intervention have failed to show that working intensively with parents for a short period of time has any effect on future abuse rates or future need for foster care.

If this kind of violence were not perpetrated on a person's biological offspring, it would land that person in jail for assault. But common sense is often overridden by faddish theories, especially when helped along with large infusions of federal cash. We now have upwards of 500,000 children lingering in foster care as a testament to the therapeutic regimen. These are children who cannot remain at home without risk to their safety, but who have not been cleared for adoption. In an attempt to redress foster-care drift, Congress passed the Adoption and Safe Families Act in 1997. Granted, the law tightens up language surrounding what constitutes reasonable efforts at keeping families together, and adds incentives to states to expedite adoptions. But, as Gelles notes, "Even with this new law, there will be problems because child welfare advocates lack the desire and the wherewithal to implement the reforms."

These advocates do not want to abandon the family preservation model, nor do they have to, thanks to Congress. In 1993, under the Omnibus Budget and Reconciliation Act, Congress gave the Clinton administration $930 million in new funding for states to implement family support and family preservation services until 2002. The administration heralded the funding as one of its crowning achievements, and indeed it was. It was the first federal infusion of money into the child welfare system in almost twenty years. In 1997, Congress reauthorized funding for another five years.

Child advocates, who actively lobbied for the reauthorization, seduced Congress into thinking that family preservation was family-friendly. How many more dead Pixleys will it take to persuade Congress otherwise?

"[Adoption] is the best of the available alternatives for children who have been subjected to abuse or neglect."

Policies Encouraging Adoption Should Be Strengthened

Elizabeth Bartholet

Adoption is the best option for abused and neglected children, argues Elizabeth Bartholet in the following viewpoint. Archaic policies that discourage the adoption of abused children because they are often older or damaged should be replaced with policies that encourage adoption of these children because adoption helps them recover and heal, contends Bartholet. She claims that potential adoptive parents want to adopt children of all races, ages, and abilities. Bartholet is an adoptive mother, a professor at Harvard Law School, and author of *Nobody's Children: Abuse and Neglect, Foster Drift, and the Adoption Alternative*, from which the following viewpoint was taken.

As you read, consider the following questions:
1. According to Bartholet, what have drug experts been saying about the adoptability of "crack babies"?
2. What does the author conclude from studies showing that children adopted as infants do better than children adopted when they are older?
3. What does the author suggest be done to expand the adoptive parent pool?

There is a lot of positive talk about adoption today, and some action. One can easily get the sense that a revolution is in the works. President Bill Clinton announced his Adoption 2002 initiative, calling for a doubling in the number of children adopted out of foster care. Congress has passed in 1996 and 1997 several pieces of legislation designed to promote adoption. New federal laws ban racial barriers to adoption, limit the excesses of family-preservation policies, encourage child welfare agencies to move more children at earlier stages into adoptive homes, and encourage potential adoptive parents by giving them tax credits for adoption expenses. State and local leaders have initiated reforms to place renewed emphasis on children's safety and welfare, and to make adoption a higher policy priority. And since 1996 the number of adoptions has been rising, with some states showing dramatic increases.

Expanding the Adoption Options

Today's talk of adoption, and some new initiatives in the works, raise the hope that our society might be ready to make genuine changes in its child welfare system, taking adoption seriously for the first time as an option for children whose parents are not capable of parenting. But it will take a lot of work to turn that hope into reality.

Estimates indicate that as of 1998 roughly 110,000 children in foster care had been freed for adoption, or had an adoption plan—about 20 percent of those in out-of-home care. Fifty-nine percent of these children are African-American, 29 percent are white, 10 percent are Hispanic, and 2 percent are of other races or ethnicities. But the need for adoption cannot be measured by these numbers. Many children are being kept in their families and in foster care, and shuffled back and forth between the two, for whom adoption should be considered, but is not. The claim has been that adoption wouldn't be good for them—that children are almost always best off with their parents. The assumption has been that adoption wouldn't be possible anyway—that the homes just aren't there for the black children, the damaged children, and the older children that dominate the foster care population.

Adoption Works

The evidence is clear that adoption works, and that it is the best of the available alternatives for children who have been subjected to abuse or neglect. This is true in terms of all the measures social scientists use to assess well-being, including measures of self-esteem and outcome measures related to later education, employment, crime and the like. It is also true in terms of abuse and neglect rates. Indeed, adopted children are less likely to suffer child abuse than is the norm in the general population of children raised by their biological parents.

Family preservationists' claim that adoption harms children by depriving them of their family and roots relies on speculative theories that adoptees suffer from "genealogical bewilderment" and the like. But empirical studies that assess how carefully selected samples and control groups of children actually fare in life, based on all the measures of human well-being that social scientists have devised, reveal no damage suffered by virtue of transferring children from their biological parents to adoptive parents. Children adopted early in infancy do essentially as well, on measures of self-esteem, attachment, and performance, as children in the general population. These studies confirm that what is central to children's welfare is that they be placed in an appropriately nurturing permanent home as early in life as possible.

Can Adoption Work for Today's Foster Care Population?

Adoption skeptics say no. They say that the children in foster care are too damaged, and many of them too old, for adoption to work. They point to the numbers who are born impaired by drugs and alcohol, the numbers who suffer from physical and mental disabilities, the numbers who have been subjected to extreme forms of abuse and neglect, and the numbers who are in their teens, having first suffered harm in their original homes, followed by many years adrift in the foster care system, or moving back and forth from foster homes to their homes of origin. They argue that while adoption might work for healthy infants, it can't work for these children. They note that significant numbers of adoptions from foster care "disrupt," with the children sent back from their adoptive homes into the foster care system. They claim that the only solutions for this damaged, older population of children lie in renewed emphasis on family preservation, on long-term foster care or guardianship, and on group or institutional homes.

The Promise of Adoption

We know it makes a difference for children to have permanent loving homes. It's not only research that tells us this; we know it by our intuition, by our own experience and we have all seen it firsthand. It was here in [the East Room of the White House in 1995] that a young woman named Deanna—a child waiting to be adopted in foster care—stood up and read a poem about what she wanted in life, and it wasn't real complicated. It is what all of us want. I'm happy that because of that event here in the East Room, she was able to meet a family who did adopt her. And I saw her last year at an event in Kansas City and almost didn't recognize her—from a shy, withdrawn 13-year-old, she had blossomed into a cheerful, outgoing, confident teenager with a brilliant smile.

Hillary Rodham Clinton, "Remarks at Adoption Bill Signing," November 19, 1997.

But the evidence indicates that adoption can and does work for children who are damaged and for children who are older. These children do have extra-ordinary needs. Most of them are far more likely to find the extra-ordinary parenting they require to overcome their history and heal their injuries in the adoptive parent population than in the families that subjected them to abuse and neglect, or in temporary foster care, or in institutional care.

A significant percentage of today's foster care and group home population are infants, many of whom were born showing the effects of their mother's use of alcohol and drugs during pregnancy. Many were removed as a result of their parents' substance abuse and related maltreatment during the period soon after birth. Drug experts have been arguing for years that "crack babies" and other infants whose mothers used licit and illicit drugs during pregnancy have a variety of special needs requiring special care, but that with that care they can flourish. These experts have advocated vigorously against simply writing off this generation of children and have testified specifically to their adoptability.

Studies of children who have suffered enormous emotional damage as a result of abuse and neglect, or wartime atrocities, show that adoption has the capacity to help many such children heal and recover, so that they can lead essentially normal lives. Adoption critics point to the adoption disruption statistics, but given the damage that so many foster care children have suffered, the fact that only roughly 10 percent of the adoptions out of the foster care system disrupt should be seen as a mark of the success achieved in these adoptive relationships. Studies of special-needs adoptions generally show that these adoptive families form the same kind of loving, committed, and satisfying family relationships as those formed in other adoptive families.

It is true that some older children in foster care have developed meaningful ties with biological parents, but adoption need not destroy such ties. There is an increasing tendency toward openness in adoption which would allow children to gain the permanence and committed parenting of an adoptive family, while maintaining healthy links with their family of origin.

A Better Option

It is also true that adoption works better for children when they are placed in infancy and when they have not been horribly damaged by abuse and neglect, or by the inconsistency and uncertainty in parenting arrangements characteristic of foster care. Adoption studies regularly confirm that age at the time of placement is the key predictor for how well adopted children will do. This is no surprise. And it is obviously no argument for giving up on adoption as a solution for the foster care population. Adoption will still work better for most foster children than any other option, although it is undoubtedly true that some children are so damaged by the maltreatment they suffered or by their experience in the child welfare system that they have to be relegated to institutional care.

These adoption studies *are* an argument for moving children out of their biological homes and on to adoptive homes as soon as it is reasonably clear that they are not likely to receive the kind of care from their parents that they need to thrive. Delay in adoption may not necessarily permanently destroy children. But abuse and neglect combined with foster drift injure children in ways that not only cause suffering but also damage their life prospects, diminishing the chances for them to flourish in the way that children adopted as infants typically do flourish. All too many foster children today *are* older and *have* suffered damage, and *do* as a result have diminished life prospects even in adoption. But these are realities that are in our power to change.

Can Adoptive Families Be Found for Today's Foster Care Population?

Adoption skeptics say no. They argue that potential adoptive parents are limited in number and interested only in healthy infants, and that the whites who make up most of the adoptive parent pool are not interested in the nonwhite children who make up most of the foster care pool.

The reality is that we have done more to drive prospective parents away from the foster care system than to draw them in. We could expand the existing parent pool by recruiting broadly; now we recruit on the most limited basis. We could socialize prospective parents in ways that would open their minds to the idea of parenting children born to other parents and other racial groups, and children who have physical and mental disabilities; for the most part we now do just the opposite.

Skeptics talk as if the number of adoptive parents and the nature of their interests were fixed in stone. In fact the "demand" for adoption is extremely malleable. What exists today is a reality that our social policies have created. History demonstrates our power to reshape this reality. Prior to the mid-nineteenth century there was no apparent interest in adoption, because there was no legal mechanism enabling adoption. It took legislative and administrative action setting up an adoption system before adoptive parents could step forward, but now that such a system has been created we have well over 100,000 adoptions per year, more than half of which are adoptions by nonrelatives. Prior to World War II there was no apparent interest in international adoption, but now that systems have been set up enabling prospective parents to adopt children from abroad, many thousands of foreign children per year come into the United States to be adopted by U.S. citizens—15,774 in fiscal year 1998. Until a couple of decades ago, the only children considered adoptable were healthy infants. Now that efforts have been made to recruit parents for children with disabilities, there are waiting lists for Down's Syndrome children and for other children who used to be relegated to institutional care. Even children with extreme disabilities have been placed by child welfare agencies that have made the effort to reach out to locate and educate potential adopters. NACAC—the North American Council on Adoptable Children—says that *no child* in the foster care system should be considered unadoptable.

The potential pool of adoptive parents is enormous—it dwarfs the pool of waiting children. About 1.2 million women are infertile and 7.1 percent of married couples, or 2.1 million. The infertile are potentially a significant resource for children in need of homes, but at present only a limited number of them adopt. It is even more rare for the fertile to think of adoption as a way to build, or add to, their family. About 1 percent of women age 18–44, or 500,000, are currently seeking to adopt. Only 0.2 percent, or 100,000, had applied to an adoption agency. It is safe to assume that millions more would have pursued adoption had our social policies encouraged rather than discouraged them.

Encouraging New Attitudes

Ours is a society that glorifies reproduction, drives the infertile to pursue treatment at all costs, socializes them to think of adoption as a second-class form of parenting to be pursued only as a last resort, and regulates adoption in a way that makes it difficult, degrading, and expensive. We could instead encourage not only the infertile but the fertile to think of adoption as a normal way to build their families. We now ask young couples when they are going to have their first baby. We could ask them when they are thinking of expanding their family, and whether they are thinking about adoption or procreation or both. We could encourage all adult members of our society to think that their responsibility as members of the national community includes caring for the youngest members of that community when care is needed.

Other countries and cultures provide evidence that our society's current attitudes are not genetically determined. Radical change is possible. In Africa and many other countries it is common for the larger community to assume responsibility for children whose parents cannot care for them. Churches and social welfare agencies have found that when they reach out to the African-American community, asking for people to step forward to provide foster and adoptive homes, they have had significant success in recruiting parents. African-Americans have recently been adopting at roughly the same rate as whites, which is dramatic evidence of the impact of socialization and recruitment, since blacks are congregated disproportionately at the bottom of the socioeconomic ladder and would not be expected to volunteer for adoptive parenthood at the same rates as those more privileged.

Questioning Racial Policies

Adoption skeptics say that whites are not interested in adopting the children in the foster care system. But we have done little to recruit adoptive parents among the relatively privileged white middle class. Instead we have told them that they may not be allowed to adopt the children of color who make up roughly two-thirds of the foster care group, and that they are guilty of racial genocide if they try. We have told them that if they want to adopt the waiting white children, they will be subject to more extensive parental fitness screening and other bureaucratic manipulations than they would face if they chose to adopt healthy infants through private agencies.

Race does matter to many adoptive parents in today's world. But our state welfare agencies have been telling adoptive parents that race *should* matter. When white parents have stepped forward to ask for black children they have often been asked why they would want to do such a thing. Written and unwritten policies have prevented whites from adopting transracially. Despite this negative conditioning, whites continue to express interest in doing so. When asked by one state welfare agency whether they would be willing to adopt children of color from the foster care system, roughly one-sixth of the waiting white prospective adopters answered yes. Many whites are adopting transracially in the private adoption system, where state barriers don't stand in the way. Many others adopt internationally, where most children are identifiable as ethnically different from their parents, and many are black and brown skinned. It is obvious that many whites would adopt from the foster care system if only we would eliminate the racial barriers, as the federal government's Multiethnic Placement Act (MEPA) legislation now commands be done. If we were to affirmatively socialize whites to believe that they *should* consider adopting children of color we could expect to increase the numbers of potential adopters exponentially.

Recruiting Parents

Age and disability also matter to many potential adopters. But we have made enormous progress in the last couple of decades in finding homes for older children and for children with physical and mental disabilities, simply because we have begun to recruit actively for those homes. Our recruitment efforts so far have been extremely limited, reaching out to only a small portion of the potential parent pool. We have failed to recruit significantly beyond the community of color and beyond the working-class white community. We have failed thus to recruit among those who might be expected, on the basis of their relative privilege, to be in the best position to reach out to give to those most in need.

We could also change the current reality by changing the social policies that keep children in damaging homes and in foster care for years—policies that, in effect, *require* that children suffer the physical and mental damage that we bemoan as making placement difficult. If we take the mandate of the 1997 Adoption and Safe Families Act seriously, and move children more swiftly out of homes in which they suffer harm, we will begin to address the problem that many claim stands in the way of finding adoptive homes.

"By reimbursing the states, the federal government has rewarded a growth in the size of the [adoption] program—not the program's effective care or placement of children."

Policies Encouraging Adoption Are Often Unfair

Dara Colwell

In the following viewpoint, Dara Colwell argues that adoption policies such as the Adoption and Safe Families Act of 1997 have given child protective services more power to remove children from their homes while limiting parents' ability to keep them. State agencies are motivated to terminate parental rights and expedite adoption because they receive money when they increase adoptions, she contends. Moreover, Colwell claims, parents are given little time to prove they should be reunited with their children, and poor, single parents have few resources to counter the child abuse allegations that resulted in their children's removal. Colwell is a freelance writer who lives in Brooklyn, New York.

As you read, consider the following questions:
1. In Colwell's opinion, why does Jennifer believe the system stole her son from her?
2. As reported by the author, why are the first hours a child is placed in protective custody the most critical assessment period in the foster care process?
3. What does Colwell claim the Adoption and Safe Families Act has done with infants and toddlers who are removed from their homes and placed in foster care?

In Adam Celaya's bedroom, thick-wheeled, plastic toy trucks with green decals sit piled in the corner, surrounded by stuffed Elmo and Tigger dolls of varying sizes. Stacked on an overstuffed bookshelf are several baby pictures: a bird's eye view of the newborn wrapped in hospital blankets, Adam at three months old, eyes wide but still unfocused, the toddler at his second Halloween, sloped across a giant pumpkin. On the nightstand facing the boy's bed stands a shrine where several muted brown and pink glass candles dedicated to Saint Anthony, protector of children, softly flicker. Their slight aroma fills the tiny room with an unspoken and solemn air. Sandwiched between the candles, is yet another photograph of Adam, an adorable and handsome 11-month-old boy, now with a full head of hair, who pouts shyly for the camera. His mother, Jennifer Celaya, turns a candle around to display the prayer on its back: "Oracion al sagrado corazon de Jesus," she mouths silently— prayer to the heart of Jesus. "It guides me through this," she says, breaking into a pragmatic tone. "It keeps hope."

A Son Is Taken from Home

Jennifer's son has been missing from this room and her life for more than two years. He was taken from her father's East San Jose, California, home by strangers on a Wednesday in June 1998 as Jennifer and family members looked on in shock.

In the months that have passed, she has heard Adam is living with a family somewhere in Santa Clara County—probably Gilroy, California. She has heard that he is "doing well." But these scraps of information that trickle down to her via the authorities are of little comfort. Celaya, an attractive Latina with heavily lined almond-shaped eyes and a dogged determination beyond her 18 years, hasn't given up fighting for her son.

With dozens of photocopied newsletters doled out in court parking lots, hundreds of phone calls to county offices, and visits all over the valley, Jennifer has spent every spare moment trying to get Adam back.

But like many young Latina mothers, with few resources and no husband, Jennifer will probably fail. Like hundreds of children in Santa Clara County and beyond, Adam Celaya was taken by Child Protective Services and placed on the fast-track for permanent adoption under a new law designed to keep children from "languishing in the system." The new system offers substantial financial rewards to counties—a kind of bounty from the federal government. And Jennifer believes the system stole her son from her not because she was an unfit mother, but because she didn't have the financial resources to defend herself. Basically, she thinks, they stole Adam—repeatedly described as an "adorable" and "adoptable child"—because they could.

A Family Feud

What happened midday June 3, 1998, in a cramped cottage tucked behind a house skirting the driveway, was a typical feud for a family whose explosive rage, bickering and jealousy were well known within Child Protective Services. The San Jose Police Department responded to a family disturbance on North 13th street, at the home of Adam Celaya Sr., Jennifer's father and Adam's grandfather. The 911 call, placed by Jennifer, would forever change the 16-year-old's life and the life of her young son.

Jennifer and her oldest sister Michelle, whose volatile relationship was marked by bitter and unpredictable outbursts, both lived with their father after their mother, Frances Barragan, had kicked Michelle out of her home. "That was what her mom did, whenever she got mad at one of her kids," the social worker commented in the court report. The two girls, Michelle's two toddlers and Adam all shared the tiny bedroom at the front of the house.

The constant tension and fighting between the girls "over clothing, children or nothing at all," according to court records, had escalated that morning when an acquaintance, Sasha, entered the house. Encouraged by Michelle, who heatedly threatened to "kick [Jennifer's] ass," Sasha, who had bounced a check Jennifer deposited for her weeks earlier, joined in the bullying as Barragan watched, shouting obscenities from the adjoining room.

As the argument spiraled out of control, Jennifer, who had been feeding Adam and still held him in her arms, was aware that he might be in danger. She suddenly set the baby, who she claims was eight inches from the kitchen floor, down to protect him. But, according to the police report and subsequent court documents, this is where accounts of the event greatly diverge. Barragan, who was noted by a nurse working closely with Jennifer since Adam's birth as being "inherently invested in her [Jennifer's] failure," stated to police that Jennifer lifted Adam "4 to 5 feet . . . above her waist and threw him to the ground." Her bad-tempered daughter, she claimed, had become "enraged."

In the same report, Barragan stated that months earlier she had seen her daughter shove Adam so hard in his stroller that he had smashed into a wall. But according to court documents, "Michelle had been present [at the incident and] Ms. Barragan had not." After taking Barragan's statement, the reporting officer immediately contacted the child abuse unit.

"I did not drop my son. I did not drop my son on purpose," Celaya, in boxer shorts and a velvet T-shirt, cried to the responding officer, visibly upset. "How was I going to defend myself?"

A Violent Family History

Jennifer herself was extremely familiar with Child Protective Services. She had been "protected" by them 17 times by the time she was 14—for neglect, physical and sexual abuse in the home where she grew up, battery and several suicide attempts by her mentally-ill mother, Frances, diagnosed as suffering from "a psychotic disorder with dissociative features." Jennifer's dense probation reports detailed a slew of chronic and uncontrollable behaviors: aggressive fighting, pushing and shoving, abusive language, gang involvement, possession of stolen goods. Between school age and high school, she repeatedly ran away from group homes where she was placed and lived, at times, on the streets.

Jennifer admits all of this readily, with great regret. She claims that after a final and drawn-out stint at a girls' ranch, she had emerged prepared to change her life. And once she became pregnant, her decision to turn away from her past was final.

Before Adam's birth, she had her tattoos removed; she entered a teen parenting program. Celaya's public health nurse,

Jane Bernard, who visited weekly, wrote that Jennifer's "entire identity focused on being a good mother." But the reporting officer responding to the family disturbance in East San Jose that morning observed Jennifer differently. "The suspect (does) not appear to have any regard for her child's well-being," Officer Hough wrote, noting that Celaya held her son as if he were a "nuisance."

Child Protective Services Passes Judgment

The police officer's observation in this case carried great weight. Celaya was cited for using excessive force in dropping Adam. Her son, then 13 months old, was placed in protective custody and admitted to the children's shelter that afternoon. According to the Little Hoover Commission Report, Restructuring Foster Care in California, these hours are crucial: deciding whether a case is indeed child abuse constitutes the most critical assessment period in the foster care process. For, "in the words of more than one program manager," the report reads, "'once you are in the system you are in for life.'"

However, the doctor's diagnosis of Adam at the children's shelter was that the child was uninjured. He was pronounced a "well-baby" on the report filed with Child Protective Services. "No bruises noted," the examiner wrote next to a sketch, which only detailed a rare bluish-gray birthmark, known as a Mongolian birthmark, on the child's posterior, which Adam had been born with, and nothing else.

As Adam's case weaved through a progression of juvenile dependency hearings, addressing his mother's past and future visitation rights, grandmother Frances Barragan sat side-by-side with her daughter. On one occasion, Barragan, a heavy-set woman who speaks quickly and breathlessly, was asked to leave the courtroom. She sat in the lobby. "They said there were conflicts every time I came around," she says. "I'm supposed to be a bad person."

Barragan later admitted to Jennifer that she had been wrong. But she insists the police report was a lie. "They [wrote] it in a different way," she says without hesitation. But it was too late—Adam had already entered the system. And the system, which had witnessed the previous generation of

Celaya children loop through Child Protective Services with dizzying frequency, had already passed judgment on Jennifer's past.

"If Adam is to have any opportunity to avoid repeating his family's generational dysfunction and enmeshment," the court papers read, "he must be provided Court intervention."

Expediting Adoptions

Leroy Martin, director of the Department of Family and Children's Services, doesn't sound like a dogmatic and over-burdened county official. He speaks as casually as his simple gray suit, touching on 30 years experience working in social services.

Martin has seen political trends within the child welfare system come and go. But over the last few years, there has been a substantial cultural change. "The philosophy," he says, cutting to the core of the shift, "is to expedite adoption and increase permanency for children."

Where the emphasis was once on "reunification," with the natural parents if possible, Martin explains, the trend now is toward adoption. Rather than allowing children to languish for years in foster care—commonly referred to as "foster drift"—there has been a dramatic push to find permanent homes for children, especially young ones, who are referred to as "highly adoptable." This is how Adam has been repeatedly described by his social workers.

With the implementation of the federal Adoption and Safe Families Act (ASFA) introduced by President Bill Clinton and passed in 1997, child protection has become big business. The drive of the initiative—to offer states cash bonuses for each child that is adopted out of foster care—is further underscored by an ultimate goal to double adoptions by the year 2002.

Rewarding Adoptions

"What California seeks to do," says Linda Riley, public information officer at California's Department of Social Services, "is reward counties that increase the number of adoptions."

In general, states earn $4,000 for each child adopted from foster care and an additional $2,000 for each "special needs" child. In order to be eligible for incentive payments, each state must increase its adoptions. If it doesn't, the state receives nothing.

What's more, incentive payments are only based on the number of adoptions that exceed the average of the previous three years. So, for example, if that number averages 500 adoptions and the current number is 600, the state receives incentive payments for 100 adoptions. Simply put, increased adoptions mean more money.

Graston. © by Graston/Rothco. Reprinted with permission.

In 1999, according to the state's Department of Social Services, Santa Clara County received $156,349 in federal adoption incentive funds.

"It's a bonus, it's a plus," Martin says openly. "But I don't think it drives our agency." The drive, he says, is based on the need and the number of children, "whether the money is there or not."

Terminating Parental Rights

The federal legislation not only granted cash incentives, but it also shortened reunification times, allowing counties further options for terminating parental rights. Once Celaya was charged with failure to protect her son from a verbally abusive environment, she had—under the newly enacted law—six months to reunite with her child. Whereas the old reunification period was 18 months—a period frequently extended in the past—parents now have one year to rehabilitate themselves or lose their child. If the child is under three, as was the case with Adam, that period has been shortened to six months. And yet another law, a policy referred to as concurrent planning, allows social workers to begin planning immediately for adoption—even as parents struggle to regain their children. . . .

Since the Adoptions and Safe Families Act was passed, adoptions in the county have more than doubled to 191 between 1998 and 2000, and the caseload has tripled, according to Michelle Swalley, spokesperson for the Department of Social Services. Of the 2,797 children in the county's foster care system in 2000, Swalley says, 300 are available for adoption in any given month.

While ASFA's intent—to address the plight of children stuck in long-term foster care and reduce their numbers—has put more teeth into time frames and increased the actual number of adoptions, "unadoptable" children remain in foster care. The legislation's stated primary goal is to promote child safety and family reunification, but by reimbursing the states, the federal government has rewarded a growth in the size of the program—not the program's effective care or placement of children.

Instead, the most adoptable age group—infants and toddlers—has been jettisoned straight into the fast track, while older children still linger.

A Poor Track Record

According to a 1992 investigative report by the Santa Clara County grand jury, which examined the practices of the local Department of Family and Children Services, the county's child welfare agency has an inconsistent track record. "It appears that there may be a tendency to jump to an unwarranted conclusion," the report reads. While the jury concluded that the majority of reports of child abuse were indeed valid, it cautioned that it "is not as confident of the department's ability to identify and dispose of these cases."

"Child Protective Services drops the ball on cases that desperately need it while intervening in those that don't," summarizes Liz Shivell at the Legal Aid Society, which represents indigent parents. Shivell has worked as a juvenile dependency attorney for 19 years. "The joke is, if the client isn't bleeding, forget it."

The changes in the law, while correcting some problems, have posed new questions that are difficult for many to answer. Even Gary Proctor, whose legal firm Juvenile Defenders represents parents in dependency court, hasn't reached a definitive conclusion. "This six month period of time is, in many instances, impossible for a parent to meet," Proctor acknowledges. "You have to ask yourself is the child's best interest served by having no chance of ever being reunited with [its] natural parent versus being in a permanent home in six months? Well," he says, pausing deliberately, "I don't have an answer for that."

Working Hard for Reunification

The next six months were Jennifer's proving ground. In order for Celaya to reunite with Adam, she had to successfully follow a case plan supervised by her social worker. Celaya, who insisted she would do whatever it took to get her son back, readily complied. The 16-year-old balanced school, a part-time job at Target to pay for her rent, multiple parenting classes, psychological counseling, and random drug testing.

She began talking about her case and carrying with her a thick stack of documents bound by a weathered manila folder, which ripped as she added to its weight. The dog-eared documents were a chronological journal of her life with Adam: their cases in juvenile court, social workers' notes, hundreds of office-visit slips from Santa Clara Valley Medical Center, testament to her trips there with Adam for asthma, ear infections and anemia. There were glowing letters from Jane Bernard, the public health nurse who tracked

Jennifer's parenting over the years, the most recent dated March 17, 2000.

"You know, Jennifer, that I think that you have had tremendous obstacles thrown in your path . . . obstacles that would have totally discouraged many young, single mothers like you," Bernard wrote. "I rarely see someone your age, with a family as non-supportive as yours is, keep trying to reach their goals with the strength that you show everyday."

Drawing Conclusions from Patchy Evidence

As Celaya struggled to fulfill her responsibilities, several things happened to swing her fate. Almost two months into her case, Sallie Bearden was replaced by Cheryl Brown, the social worker who would follow Celaya's case through the next eight months. Brown strictly adhered to concurrent planning guidelines and actively encouraged Celaya's oldest sister Irene to adopt the child.

Jennifer also tested positive for methamphetamine use five times in a three-month period under a relatively new drug-testing method called the PharmChem patch. Child Protective Services is the only county agency to employ the method, which has been increasingly condemned by critics as unreliable due to its high rate of false-positives. While Brown mentions, in the court papers terminating Celaya's rights to regain her son, her concerns over the mother's "continued positive drug tests," Celaya says she never learned of the results until her trial and there was no mechanism to challenge the results.

Celaya adamantly denies she took drugs. Several months after the trial, when Celaya demanded copies of her tests, Brown noted in her work log that she could "possibly" obtain copies. Celaya says she never received any.

At the same time, Adam began displaying aggressive behavior at his day care. The child began kicking and biting other day-care children as well as using swear words. His day-care provider said Adam seemed to be acting out the emotional distress, uncertainty and conflicting family loyalties his placement had created. This, to Brown, who wrote that Adam was "presenting as a very disturbed child," was a big concern. Coupled with Jennifer's positive drug tests, Brown reached only one conclusion at the child's six-month hearing in January, 1999: Jennifer should not be reunited with her son.

As it turns out, there was one last chance for Jennifer, but no one told her about it. There is a little-known seven-day window of appeal for parents who have lost reunification rights. And even workers within the juvenile dependency court clerk's office are poorly informed about it.

Until May of 1999, Adam remained in his aunt Irene's care. Everything seemed to be going smoothly until Adam began acting up again in daycare. As the social worker looked into why his aggressive behavior had resurfaced, she discovered that Jennifer had been allowed unauthorized contact with the child. Irene, swamped by responsibilities for her own children, had allowed Jennifer to take Adam to medical appointments and even arrange for child care. Jennifer denied the charges of unauthorized contact. But Brown pieced it together in a way that made sense to her: she believed that the child's increasing exposure to his family members, whose verbal abuse marked their interaction, was putting the child at risk. Adam was again placed into protective custody. The next step was foster placement. Within weeks of foster placement, the new family expressed an interest in adopting Adam.

A few weeks later, in June, 1999, Jennifer lost custody of her son.

"Each year at least a million children are beaten in the name of 'discipline,' billions of dollars are spent on child abuse prevention, and the system devised to protect children fails."

Disciplinary Spanking Should Be Banned

Nadine Block

Corporal punishment such as spanking can lead to child abuse and should therefore be banned, claims Nadine Block in the following viewpoint. Support for a ban on spanking comes from research showing that children who are spanked display aggressive and other antisocial behaviors, suggests Block. Moreover, she argues, research demonstrates that the children of parents who reason with them as a method of discipline score higher on cognitive tests than those who are disciplined using corporal punishment. Block is director of the Center for Effective Discipline and co-chair of End Physical Punishment of Children (EPOCH).

As you read, consider the following questions:

1. In Block's opinion, what provides the strongest and most enduring support for corporal punishment?
2. According to the author, what are some of the conclusions drawn by authorities who research the effects of corporal punishment?
3. What does the author say has been the result of banning corporal punishment in Sweden?

Nadine Block, "Abandon the Rod and Save the Child," *Humanist*, vol. 60, March 2000, pp. 5–12. Copyright © 2000 by the American Humanist Association. Reproduced by permission of the author.

Corporal punishment is the intentional infliction of physical pain for a perceived misbehavior.

It includes spanking, slapping, pinching, choking, and hitting with objects. The practice is not permitted against prison or jail inmates, military personnel, or mental patients; nor is it allowed against a spouse, a neighbor, or even a neighbor's dog. Instead, in the United States, corporal punishment is legally preserved only for children.

Children have been the victims since early colonial times and today remain so with the support of the courts and a significant percentage of the citizenry. Each year at least a million children are beaten in the name of "discipline," billions of dollars are spent on child abuse prevention, and the system devised to protect children fails. Yet, the subject is a divisive one that often pits generation against generation and family member against family member.

Incurring God's Wrath?

One reason for this divisiveness is corporal punishment's roots in theology. The strongest and most enduring support for the practice comes from the Bible, particularly the Old Testament. Many fundamentalist, evangelical, and charismatic Protestants use scripture to justify their use of corporal punishment to develop obedience and character in children. Their position is that God wills and requires it in order to obtain his blessing and approval; to not physically punish children for misbehavior will incur God's wrath.

For example, in "The Correction and Salvation of Children" on the Way of Life website (wayoflife.org/~dcloud/), the Reverend Ronald E. Williams of the Believers Baptist Church in Winona Lake, Indiana, contends that the biblical "rod of correction" is a physical object, in most cases a wooden paddle for use in spanking a child's buttocks; any unwillingness to use physical correction is "child abuse." While he recognizes that using an object to hit a child increases the chance of injury, and while he cautions that bruising is not the goal of "correction," Williams counsels parents not to be overly concerned if bruising happens:

> But these opponents of God's methods may object, "What you are suggesting will hurt the child and may even bruise

him!" My response would be, "That is correct." A child may in fact be bruised by a session of difficult correction. In fact, the Lord has already anticipated this objection and has discussed it briefly in the Scriptures. "The blueness of a wound cleanseth away evil: so do stripes the inward parts of the belly" (Proverbs 20:30). One may say, "That is talking about a child who has bruised himself in an accident at play." No, the latter part of the verse explains that God is giving this passage in the context of physical chastening for correction. God makes the point that if a child is bruised during one of these sessions of correction that a parent should not despair but realize that the blueness of the wound cleanses away the evil heart of rebellion and willful stubbornness that reside in that depraved little body.

Williams also believes that corporal punishment should begin early in life:

> My wife and I have a general goal of making sure that each of our children has his will broken by the time he reaches the age of one year. To do this, a child must receive correction when he is a small infant.

However, the Reverend Thomas E. Sagendorf, a Methodist pastor and member of the advisory board of the Center for Effective Discipline's program, End Physical Punishment of Children (EPOCH)—USA, points out that Old Testament scripture can also be used to justify slavery, suppression of women, polygamy, incest, and infanticide. So, like many believers in the Bible, Sagendorf prefers to look for guidance on disciplining children in the New Testament. There, he says, children are shown great love and compassion, and violence is not tolerated.

The Religious Roots of Corporal Punishment

Rutgers University historian Philip Greven, in his 1992 book *Spare the Child: The Religous Roots of Punishment and the Psychological Impact of Physical Abuse*, paints a deeply disturbing picture of religion's influence on discipline and the consequences of that influence. Examining the effects of corporal punishment on the American psyche and culture, Greven reminds us that, although some of the fundamentalist Protestant groups are most outspoken in defending corporal punishment, they have a great deal of secular support.

He says centuries of strong Protestant traditions begun in

Europe have been infused into modern U.S. law, education, and the behavioral sciences. The beliefs that children are inherently bad, that their wills must be broken, that their behavior must be controlled all have theological sources. Whether it was overtly or tacitly endorsed in our individual experiences, corporal punishment is deeply rooted in our psyches and, therefore, not easily or willingly examined. The first step in changing our consciousness and behavior toward children, Greven advises, is to confront the repressed fundamentalism in ourselves.

Challenging Attitudes

Fortunately, a growing willingness to challenge ingrained attitudes has resulted in a waning societal acceptance of corporal punishment. For example, almost universally accepted in the 1950s, the practice has decreased each generation since. In 1985 only five states had banned it in public schools; today twenty-seven states have done so. Even in those states that still allow corporal punishment, many of the larger cities have banned it. In 1991 the American Academy of Pediatrics (AAP) called on parents, educators, legislators and other adults to seek the legal prohibition by all states of corporal punishment in schools. Unable to hush pro-spanking sentiments within its own ranks, however, the AAP stopped short of calling for a complete ban in 1998. Instead it recommended that its members encourage and assist parents in developing nonviolent responses to misbehavior.

The changing perception of corporal punishment is being helped along by research in the field of physical abuse. Much of it is correlational and retrospective in nature, given the difficulty of designing such experiments and the abhorrence of assigning children spanking and paddling treatment. It is, however, compelling.

Greven examines the effects of corporal punishment on children in *Spare the Child* and there finds the roots of public and domestic violence. He says the religious and authoritarian nature of the practice leads children to accept violence without question and believe it is deserved. Rage unable to be expressed by a child is repressed and denied—but doesn't go away. It can later appear in the form of destructive and aggressive behavior toward others or, turned on the self, can lead to psychological problems such as depression and melancholia. Greven says many such problems can be traced to a history of pain, abuse, and suffering in childhood, and the most common source has always been corporal punishment.

Examining the Research

In his 1994 book *Beating the Devil Out of Them: Corporal Punishment in American Families*, University of New Hampshire Family Research Laboratory Co-director Murray Straus reviews the dozens of studies he has authored or coauthored that show corporal punishment contributes to interpersonal violence. Among his results, Straus found that children who were spanked regularly and severely have higher rates of hitting siblings, hitting their spouses as adults, and assaulting someone outside their family. Children who are frequently spanked for lying, cheating, hitting siblings, and being disobedient are more likely to display these kinds of antisocial behaviors.

Studies by Straus and others have also found that corporal punishment can escalate to the level of abuse prohibited by law. Since parents are more likely to spank when they are tired, stressed, depressed, and fatigued, and a majority of parents express moderate to high anger when spanking children, it is little surprise that parents who believe in corporal punishment are more likely to injure children than parents who do not. And children who are regularly spanked are more likely to continue the practice on the next generation and to show less remorse for wrongdoing as adults.

Even infrequent and moderate spanking in childhood can have deleterious effects in adult life, including a greater likelihood of depression and other psychological problems. Conversely, Straus found that children who are rarely or never spanked score higher on cognitive tests than those who are frequently spanked. He theorizes that parents who don't spank spend more time reasoning with and explaining to children, thus maximizing verbal ability.

A U.S. Department of Education survey indicates that about 500,000 students are hit each year in the nation's pub-

Mental Development with and Without Spanking

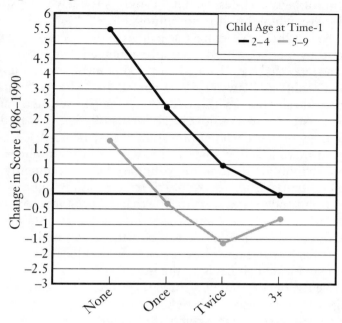

Corporal Punishment in Two Sample Weeks

Murray A. Straus, *Beating the Devil Out of Them*, 2001.

lic schools. Physical injuries, including hematomas and broken bones, have resulted from adults hitting children in school with boards—sometimes in anger and in unobserved and unsupervised settings. The National Coalition to Abolish Corporal Punishment in Schools, another program of the Center for Effective Discipline, estimates that 2 percent of children who are paddled need medical care. Twenty years of DOE surveys analyzed by the coalition and the center reveal that corporal punishment in schools is used more frequently on children with disabilities, poor children, boys, and minority children.

Ending Corporal Punishment

Despite the compelling research, the task of ending corporal punishment in the United States is a daunting one. All too often repeated by those who grew up with violence are comments like "My parents hit me because they loved me" and "I got hit because I deserved it." Progress is likely to be slow and incremental, but it is not impossible.

The last fifteen years have seen a great deal of progress on a state-by-state basis. For example, nineteen of the twenty-seven states that have banned corporal punishment in public schools did so between 1985 and 1994. The remaining twenty-three states without bans—primarily southern and southwestern states—allow local boards of education to determine whether corporal punishment may be used.

And there is a slow but steady increase in the number of those school boards adopting voluntary bans—frequently to avoid potential litigation resulting from paddling injuries. In Ohio, child advocates were unable to get a complete ban, but they got so many restrictions put into law that only forty-two out of 611 school districts report using corporal punishment. Each year a few more districts enact a local ban, making a statewide ban likely in the near future.

The use of corporal punishment in other child-caring settings (daycare centers, foster care, and institutions) varies from state to state. State regulatory agencies are moving toward complete bans, and a great deal of legislative and regulatory progress has been made since 1980 because of extensive public education campaigns.

Perhaps an easier route is to get a federal ban on corporal punishment. Schools could be prompted to comply by tying federal funding to requirements for adopting bans, as Democratic Representative Major Owens of New York attempted in the early 1990s.

The European View

In all this, the United States is taking a lesson from Europe, where corporal punishment in schools was banned long ago. Nine European countries—Austria, Croatia, Cyprus, Denmark, Finland, Italy (by court decision), Latvia, Norway, and Sweden—have banned corporal punishment in all settings, including homes.

Sweden was the first country to act. It took away parents' specific authority to use corporal punishment, then passed a comprehensive ban three years later in 1979, accompanied by a large-scale education effort. The law is generally used to require educational training of parents who hit children, but offenders can be subjected to criminal prosecution. The overall process has resulted in an overwhelming acceptance of the ban in Sweden and, more importantly, a decline in child abuse. U.S. child advocates are watching carefully as a number of countries—including Germany, Ireland, New Zealand, Switzerland, and the United Kingdom—are studying this model for possible adoption.

In Canada, an effort is underway to abolish Section 43 of the Criminal Code, which gives parents authority to use "reasonable chastisement" on children. Abolition of this section is likely to be followed by a complete ban that follows the Swedish model. Meanwhile, Susan Bitensky, a law professor and EPOCH advisory board member, has suggested criminalizing corporal punishment of children and making violators subject to the same criminal penalties imposed in adult assaults and batteries. In the winter 1998 University of Michigan Journal of Law Reform, Bitensky says such a law could be effective if accompanied by prosecutorial restraint and a strong public education program, such as that used in the Swedish model.

The most successful initiatives to end corporal punishment have included public education campaigns. With that in mind, EPOCH initiated SpankOut Day USA on April 30, 1998. Modeled after the Great American Smokeout, the annual observance seeks to bring widespread attention to the need to end corporal punishment of children as an important way of addressing the U.S. child abuse and neglect emergency. Between 1998 and 2000, more than 400 informational events were held for parents and educators.

EPOCH emphasizes discipline as teaching rather than punishment. While its current activities are largely educational in nature, the organization also seeks legal reform. An important step forward in that effort would be the adoption of the United Nations Convention on the Rights of the Child, which provides a legal basis for improving the lives of children throughout the world. Specifically, the international agreement requires ratifying countries to take measures to protect children from abuse and neglect and strongly supports nonviolent discipline of children. The United States and Somalia are the only countries that haven't adopted the convention. Many of the nations that have are using it to support their efforts to ban corporal punishment in homes.

"I support all efforts to end the physical abuse of children, but I do not think that spanking, used rarely and judiciously, is abuse."

Disciplinary Spanking Is Not Child Abuse

Okey Chigbo

In the following viewpoint, Okey Chigbo argues that spanking is not child abuse, and parents should not be afraid to discipline their children with an occasional spank. Moreover, Chigbo claims, arguments that spanking contributes to antisocial behavior and societal violence are not supported by evidence. According to the author, most parents do not like to spank their children, but under some circumstances spanking is the only disciplinary tool that works. Okey Chigbo is an editor for camagazine.com, a Canadian financial publication.

As you read, consider the following questions:

1. Why is Chigbo not comforted by claims that minor breaches of antispanking laws will not be prosecuted?
2. What conclusion does Chigbo draw from statistics on violent crime in the United States between 1985 and 1993?
3. What does the author claim antispankers forget concerning authority figures in our society?

Whenever I read something on the spanking contro-versy, I remember an incident in a downtown day care. It happened at about 6:05 p.m., five minutes past the deadline for parents to depart with their offspring. The staff was itching to leave, and an occasional dirty look aimed at a tardy parent darted through the mask of cordiality stretched across their faces. I was hurriedly helping my son put on his socks, shoes, and coat, when I heard a commotion behind me. I turned; it was another late parent walking toward us carrying a boy of about four, her arms locked firmly around his middle. He was kicking and yelling at the top of his lungs, "No! No! Put me down!" She was talking to him in the very best contemporary parenting book manner: very calmly, very firmly, not raising her voice. "It's time to go now," she said. "I've given you 20 minutes to play with the day-care toys. That's enough. Daddy's got dinner ready, and he's waiting for us at home."

She put him down by the kiddie coat rack, and knelt be-side him. He seized this brief moment of freedom to unleash a barrage of blows to her head and chest. "Let me go!" he yelled as he connected with her chin. She looked around in embarrassment. I averted my eyes. "That hurt," she said evenly, taking down his coat, "That really hurt. I don't like that." She grappled with him in a fruitless effort to force him into his coat; he wriggled out easily, shoving her face as far away from him as possible. The struggle continued for min-utes, then reached a stalemate. The day-care staff, looking on with increasing disgust and fatigue, offered such helpful comments as, "Come on Tyler. It's time to go home now."

As I left with my son, I reflected upon the spirit of the age that has blessed us with such incidents. Perhaps some non-aversive method of discipline would have made that terrible child comply with his mother's request quickly, but I cannot think of it. I am convinced that the most effective solution in that particular instance would have been a sharp, compliance-inducing swat on the bottom.

A New Definition of Spanking

But what parent does that today when people are watching? The antispanking movement has done a brilliant job propagating the view that spanking is just another form of child abuse. Normal parents are not just frightened of appearing abusive; they also fear that an occasional swat to the behind can turn their little darling into a dangerously aggressive adolescent and an incorrigibly criminal adult, as the "scientific evidence" says. In fact, the antispanking movement, and its agents in the mainstream media, has used this weak, and in some cases simply non-existent, evidence to beat parents into submission. Antispanking advocates have given us nothing more than a smattering of half-truths along with heavy smacks of propaganda.

Before I continue, let me state categorically that I reject spanking as a primary method of discipline. Let no one see this article as encouragement to parents to spank their children for every little thing. It goes without saying that I support all efforts to end the physical abuse of children, but I do not think that spanking, used rarely and judiciously, is abuse. Rather, it can be useful in some situations, with many kids.

But what is spanking? Antispankers define it as broadly as possible, not just to show that spanking causes harm, but to more easily place it on a continuum with child abuse. One antispanking article, for example, defined spanking as "any disciplinary hitting of kids that's not injurious or currently considered abusive." Note the emotive and misleading word hitting which can include punching, cuffing, boxing the ears, and slapping the face. But the meaning of the word spanking, which has remained relatively stable over the centuries, is quite different from these abusive behaviors. The English language's most authoritative source, the Oxford English Dictionary, defines the verb to spank as "To slap or smack (a person, esp. a child) with the open hand." Its earliest etymological entry, dated 1727, reads, "To spank, to slap with the open hand." Another citation from 1889 shows how it was done then (and continues to be done now): "My mother . . . lifted me cleverly [and] planted two spanks behind." In 1996, the Canadian Paediatric Society (CPS) gave a similar definition of "disciplinary spanking": "[It] is physically non-injurious, administered with an opened hand to the buttocks, and intended to modify behavior." This is the definition agreed upon by the American Academy of Pediatrics and the one I use. I reject any broader definition as an insidious effort to demonize this age-old and harmless practice.

A Movement to Criminalize Spanking

In Canada, the anispanking movement has embarked on what it hopes is a final offensive against spanking. In 1998, an advocacy group called the Canadian Foundation for Children, Youth and the Law received $45,000 from the Federal Court Challenges Program to help it mount a Charter of Rights and Freedoms challenge to Section 43 of the Criminal Code, which allows parents to use "reasonable force" in correcting their children. The foundation spearheads the Canadian branch of a North America-wide movement of liberal childcare professionals, assorted experts, and sundry kind-hearted folk that seeks to abolish every form of physical punishment aimed at children. These people are not just concerned with clear child abuse; Canadian law, they say, should not permit parents even the open-handed, non-injurious smack to a defiant child's bottom. They therefore want to repeal Section 43, not amend it. If the foundation wins, police could lay assault charges against parents who swat their four-year-old. Because the legal challenge is underway in the lower courts, the foundation's lawyers are not talking to journalists. No one knows when the process will be completed.

Many people fear that a repeal of Section 43 could criminalize a vast number of otherwise law-abiding citizens. In a 1995 letter to the *Canadian Medical Association Journal*, Dr. Bruce Williams highlights the irony: "Those who oppose the use of punishment in raising children favor the use of punishment, in the form of criminal sanctions, to deal with those who use corporal punishment on their children."

A Reason to Fear Using Discipline

Of course, propagandists for the cause deny that parents who only spank will face any criminal charges after the repeal. "Minor breaches of the law are not prosecuted," stated antispanking lawyer Corinne Robertshaw in 1997. *Toronto Star* columnist Michele Landsberg assumes, "No cop or children's aid worker is ever going to report the parent who merely spanks a toddler's bottom for darting into the road."

Really? Perhaps Robertshaw and Landsberg can explain why U.S. tourist David Peterson was charged with assault in 1994 and locked up in a London, Ontario, jail when some local do-gooder saw him spank his five-year-old daughter and reported him to the cops. Peterson was no abusive, ignorant, and drunken bully, viciously whacking his daughter indiscriminately: Described as "mild mannered" in newspaper and magazine accounts, Peterson has an MBA and is a specialist in production management. His wife, Paula, has an MA in early childhood education and was working on her doctorate at the time. Peterson had followed an established family procedure, spanking his child only after she had been given sufficient warning and had persisted in her behavior. The judge threw out the case, but if someone can be prosecuted while spanking is still legal, what will happen when it is actually illegal?

Writing in the *Canadian Paediatric Society News Bulletin*, Dr. Mervyn Fox, former chair of the CPS's Psychosocial Paediatrics Committee, gives another reason to question Robertshaw and Landsberg's assumptions: "I consult on behavioral paediatrics at a children's mental health centre in a county whose Children's Aid Society has a strong bias against any physical punishment. The society is widely regarded as punitive rather than rehabilitative, absolutist rather than allowing for individual variations. In consequence, parents are afraid to use any discipline for fear of prosecution."

Blaming Societal Violence on Spanking

Antispankers attribute much of the violence in North American society—the urban violence among youth, the vandalism, the brutal rapes—directly to the physical punishment of children. According to the doyen of antispanking advocates, University of New Hampshire sociologist Professor Murray Straus, "Although physical punishment may produce conformity in the immediate situation, in the longer run, it tends to increase the probability of deviance, including delinquency in adolescence and violent crime inside and outside the family as an adult [sic]."

The North American media seems to agree with Straus's conclusions and uncritically publishes every questionable claim. In August 1997, the journal *Archives of Pediatrics and Adolescent Medicine* published yet another study led by Straus; the study "showed" that spanking children is "a significant predictor of ASB [antisocial behavior] two years later." Every major newspaper reported it, with some running opinion pieces by self-appointed experts that said, basically, "children whose parents still swat them on the bottom will grow up to be violent monsters."

Questioning the Research

Even without a PhD in sociology, the average person, using his common sense, should be suspicious of studies that claim spanking increases societal violence. The first question the skeptic asks: Was there more violence and crime in the '50s and '60s than there is now? The answer, of course, is no. "To be sure, there is at least three times as much violent crime today as there was 30 years ago," writes Harvard's James Q. Wilson, author of *Crime and Human Nature and The Moral Sense*. But if the theory that more spanking equals more societal violence is correct, the '50s and '60s should have been a hellish period of violent crime. Parents spanked more then. According to Straus himself, 99 per cent of American parents spanked or used some form of corporal punishment in 1950; in 1999 everyone, including Straus, agrees that the use of corporal punishment and spanking has declined. Survey figures say that 70 to 90 per cent of parents now spank.

The Proper Use of Spanking

Reactive, impulsive hitting after losing control due to anger is unquestionably the wrong way for a parent to use corporal punishment. Eliminating all physical punishment in the home, however, would not remedy such explosive scenarios. It could even increase the problem. When effective spanking is removed from a parent's disciplinary repertoire, he or she is left with nagging, begging, belittling, and yelling, once the primary disciplinary measures—such as time-out and logical consequences—have failed. By contrast, if proper spanking is proactively used in conjunction with other disciplinary measures, better control of the particularly defiant child can be achieved, and moments of exasperation are less likely to occur.

Den A. Trumbull and S. DuBose Ravenel, *Family Policy*, October 1996.

A careful look at U.S. crime statistics also refutes the idea that spanking equals more societal violence. Between 1985 and 1993, violent crime actually decreased by 20 per cent among males 25 or older, while it increased 65 per cent for males 18 to 24 and by 165 per cent for 14- to 17-year-old males. So those who grew up in a period of more spanking were, and are, less violent than younger people who have grown up in a period of declining approval and practice of spanking. This does not prove that a decrease in spanking makes societies more violent, but these statistics throw cold water on any notion that blames spanking for societal violence.

Some may say, "Well, that's the U.S., they're crazier down there; there may be other reasons—availability of guns for instance—that have skewed the statistics." These doubters should consider Sweden, a historically nonviolent country and a favorite of antispanking advocates. The Swedish government outlawed spanking in 1979 and operated an extensive education program to wean parents away from corporal punishment. Since the ban, police reports of teen violence have soared sixfold, according to Statistics Sweden. "What is happening in Sweden is gang violence, mobbing as they call it over there," says non-abusive spanking researcher Dr. Robert Larzelere, a director of research at the Youth Care Building in Boys Town, Nebraska, and a vocal critic of the blanket antispanking position. "Violence has dramatically increased over the last decade or more."

A Questionable Link

Despite this evidence, antispanking advocates continue to link spanking and violence. At a 1996 corporal punishment conference, Straus cited anthropologist Ashley Montague who argued that "spanking the baby may be the psychological seed of war." In 1978, Montague gathered eight anthropologists who had studied nonviolent primitive societies such as the Fore of New Guinea and the Aborigines of Australia. These anthropologists published their accounts of primitive child-rearing practices in the book *Learning Non-Aggression*, which showed that none of these nonviolent societies spanked their children.

But Laurie J. Bauman of the department of pediatrics, Albert Einstein College of Medicine, criticized Straus's logic by pointing out that these "societal level studies cannot be used to show causality." Other factors (rather than spanking) could have made these societies nonviolent, factors like overall social attitudes and values. . . .

Is Spanking Harmful?

Within the child-development professions and among the researchers, however, a battle still rages over the meaning of corporal punishment and spanking research. On the one side are those who want all forms of corporal punishment, including spanking, banned because it is harmful and doesn't work. Anthony M. Graziano, Jessica L. Hamblen, and Wendy A. Plante write in *Pediatrics:* "It is . . . reasonable to assume the position that corporal punishment in child rearing should be discouraged because it is morally objectionable and, in any event, is not even needed." On the other side are those who do not necessarily support spanking, but they think that there is not enough evidence to demand a blanket ban, or to lecture parents on how to discipline their children. People like Boys Town's Robert E. Larzelere, or the venerable Diana Baumrind of Berkeley, who has researched child development for almost 50 years, argue that spanking is effective and not harmful to children between two and six if used sparingly to back up other non-aversive disciplinary measures. . . .

So where does rejection of their scientific claims leave the antispanking lobby? With a lot of sermonizing, loads of half-baked opinions, and very poor moral arguments. In the spring 1994 issue of *Empathic Parenting,* the journal of the Canadian Society for the Prevention of Cruelty to Children, British child psychologist Penelope Leach writes, "Spanking is wrong because we all agree that hitting people is wrong and children are people." This sort of argument may sound good on first reading, but we can't make such blanket statements because in many situations most of us agree hitting people is "necessary." If you go to a bar and start a brawl, the bouncers may use reasonable force to eject you; if you go outside and continue, the police will show up, and ask you to cease and desist. If you do not and "show verbal non-compliance," you might receive a disabling whack, delivered to the outside of the thigh with a nightstick. Comfortable middle-class anti-spankers forget that our society gives authority figures the right to use "reasonable force" to control public disturbances; similarly, in that microcosm of society, the family, the author-ity figures of the home—parents—should have the right to do the same to control the behavior of their children.

Leach's arguments get worse: "When a mugger hits an old lady for money," she writes, "or a child hits another for candy, is it any different from when a parent hits a child to get him to obey?" It's difficult to take this seriously. Unlike normal parental spanking, mugging for money and snatch-ing candy are purely egotistical acts; when responsible par-ents spank their children, they seek neither personal satis-faction nor gain: they seek to correct inappropriate behavior, for the child's ultimate benefit. In many cases, the parent is reluctant to spank, and feels terrible after doing it. Does this describe the average mugger or candy-snatching kid?

Condemning Parents Who Spank

Other antispankers argue that if we consider ourselves moral beings, we should not strike children to correct them. But parents who spank generally do so as part of a larger effort to teach children moral behavior. Antispankers argue that this is illogical, because you can't teach people not to hit oth-ers by hitting them, yet many useful, and even necessary, hu-man behaviors appear illogical on paper. We fight large con-flagrations by setting small controlled fires; in medicine, we end major pain and suffering by inflicting the relatively mi-nor pain of surgery, injection, or dental operation. Causing children minor pain to correct a larger ill is neither inher-ently immoral nor illogical.

Antispankers suggest, in place of spanking, time-outs, rea-soning, and removal of privileges. These are fine measures, which should be among every parent's disciplinary tools. But are they workable at all times and for all ages? Antispanking dogmatists stoutly insist that they are; if you point out that these measures are not working for your kid, you're simply not doing it right, you incompetent parent. But columnist John Rosemond, the bête noire of the U.S. psychological community, explains that time-outs sometimes don't work. "The letter writer advises that time-out will work if it is used consistently," he writes in one of his newspaper columns. "The problem is, one cannot use time-out consistently. It is difficult, if not impossible, to use if a behavior problem occurs away from home or when the parents are rushing out of the house to make an appointment. And children who are inclined toward misbehavior figure these things out quickly." As a parent, I wholeheartedly agree. As for reasoning, a review of studies on verbal explanation and reasoning led by Nathan J. Blum of the University of Pennsylvania School of Medicine, and published in *Pediatrics*, found that "verbal explanations and instructions are not effective in changing young children's problem behaviors."

Rather than a repeal, child-welfare advocates should call for an amendment to the Criminal Code's Section 43, to close loopholes that allow abusive parents to escape punishment. Instead of allowing parents the right to use "reasonable force"—which can be interpreted in various ways—the law could clearly specify what is acceptable and what is not. But it should not ban spanking outright.

A Minority View

I personally believe that a large number of do-gooders out there are just itching to get their hands on a legal stick with which to beat that Neanderthal pro-spanking majority among parents. A general survey of Americans shows that antispanking is the moral view of a minority of the population: The greatest supporters of antispanking are educated, white, middle-class women. I have absolutely nothing against educated, white, middle-class women; I just don't think that the morality of this minority should be imposed on the rest of us. A blanket ban will especially affect immigrants whom, I suspect, more often spank their children. Why criminalize a growing segment of our population, the majority of whom are otherwise law abiding, simply because they have a different view on how to raise decent children?

Where is all this leading? Retired Vancouver child psychiatrist Thomas P. Millar thinks that the antispanking movement is part of a wider agenda to ban all forms of punishment. It is easy to dismiss this claim until you discover that eminent antispanker Dr. Joan McCord of Temple University argues that we should question the value of all forms of punishment because they all lead to the same evil things Straus claims for spanking. The battle lines over this particular conflict have already been drawn: At a conference on Research in Discipline, held in Chapel Hill, North Carolina, in 1996, McCord declared that the research showed that all punishment is unnecessary and undesirable, while another heavyweight in the field, Berkeley's Baumrind, argued that the research showed the opposite.

If we are headed for McCord's world, we should heed the warning of that great historian of Roman affairs, Jérôme Carcopino, writing in his masterpiece *Daily Life in Ancient Rome*. He was describing the Roman Empire at the height of its prosperity and decadence, just before it embarked on its 350-year decline: "The laws had once more adapted themselves to public feeling which, condemning the atrocious severities of the past, asked . . . nothing more of paternal authority than . . . natural affection. . . . But, unhappily, the Romans failed to strike the happy mean. They were not content to lessen the old severity; they yielded to the impulse to become far too complaisant. . . . The result was that they were succeeded by a generation of idlers and wastrels."

Periodical Bibliography

The following articles have been selected to supplement the diverse views presented in this chapter.

Diana Baumrind, Robert E. Larzelere, and Philip A. Cowan — "Ordinary Physical Punishment: Is It Harmful?" *Psychological Bulletin*, 2002.

Howard A. Davidson — "Protecting America's Children: A Challenge," *Trial*, January 1999.

Tom DeLay — "Fighting for Children," *American Psychologist*, September 2000.

Joan E. Durrant — "Evaluating the Success of Sweden's Corporal Punishment Ban," *Child Abuse and Neglect*, May 1999.

Deanna S. Gomby — "Promise and Limitations of Home Visitation," *JAMA*, September 20, 2000.

Sarah McCue Horwitz, Kathleen M.B. Balestracci, and Mark D. Simms — "Foster Care Placement Improves Children's Functioning," *Archives of Pediatrics & Adolescent Medicine*, November 2001.

Marnie Ko — "Beware the 'Child Savers,'" *Alberta Report*, April 24, 2000.

Gerald Landsberg and Corrine Wattam — "Differing Approaches to Combating Child Abuse: United States vs. United Kingdom," *Journal of International Affairs*, Fall 2001.

John M. Leventhal — "The Challenges of Recognizing Child Abuse," *JAMA*, February 17, 1999.

John D. Lierman — "Spare the Children," *Religion & Society Report*, September 1999.

Brenda McGowan and Elaine M. Walsh — "Policy Challenges for Child Welfare in the New Century," *Child Welfare*, January/February 2000.

Christopher Meisenkothen — "Chemical Castration—Breaking the Cycle of Paraphiliac Recidivism," *Social Justice*, Spring 1999.

Eugene Narrett — "The Envious State: 'Mandated to Protect Children,'" *Culture Wars*, January 2000.

Eugene Narrett — "Spanking May Be a Mistake, But the State Should Stay Out," *Wanderer*, February 18, 1999.

Beverly R. Newman

"For the Love of Laura: When the Foster Care System Endangers Children," *World & I*, December 1999.

Anne Reiniger

"Reducing Child Abuse," *New York Times*, August 17, 2000.

Felicia F. Romeo

"The Educator's Role in Reporting the Emotional Abuse of Children," *Journal of Instructional Psychology*, September 2000.

Phyllis Schafly

"More Liberal Interference for Families," *Conservative Chronicle*, March 24, 1999.

Theodore J. Stein

"The Adoption and Safe Families Act: Creating a False Dichotomy Between Parents' and Children's Rights," *Families in Society: The Journal of Contemporary Human Services*, November 2000.

For Further Discussion

Chapter 1

1. The authors in this chapter discuss a variety of causes of child abuse. Some focus on the characteristics of caregivers, others focus on the characteristics of children, and still others point to societal influences. Which focus do you think is most persuasive? Which factor do you think contributes most to child abuse? Please explain.

2. The National Coalition for Child Protection Reform says that laws prohibiting neglect target poor families. How could the laws that prohibit neglect be written so as not to discriminate against poor families?

3. Julie Hudash suggests that some industries such as advertising, entertainment, and retail oversexualize children, which may entice pedophiles. Hudash argues that parents should take action to prevent their own children from being sexualized. Do you agree that protecting children from exploitation is the parent's responsibility, or should these industries be asked to take some of the responsibility? Explain.

Chapter 2

1. Stephen J. Rossetti claims that some priests accused of child sexual abuse should be returned to a limited, supervised ministry. To support his conclusion, he makes a distinction between those who abuse young children and those who abuse adolescents. Those who abuse adolescents, he argues, are more amenable to treatment. Do you think this distinction should influence whether priests are dismissed or whether they should be treated? Why or why not? Do you think the fact that Rossetti is president of a psychiatric hospital that treats clergy influences his position?

2. David McGrath focuses his argument for a zero-tolerance policy on the harm done to *current* victims, arguing that one instance of child sexual abuse does enough damage to call for immediate dismissal of offending priests. The editors of the *National Catholic Reporter*, on the other hand, focus their arguments against a zero-tolerance policy on the harm to *potential* victims, arguing that zero-tolerance policies don't lead to an understanding of why priests abuse children, knowledge necessary to prevent future abuse. Which perspective do you find most persuasive? Why?

3. Tom Barrett and Joseph J. Guido disagree on the question of whether homosexuals should be members of the priesthood. What types of evidence does each use to support his argument? Which type of evidence do you find most persuasive? Why?

Chapter 3

1. Suzanne D. DiNubile argues that the purpose of community notification laws is to protect children from child molesters. However, Robert E. Freeman-Longo discusses many instances in which innocent people have been hurt by community notification laws. Do the cases presented by Freeman-Longo convince you that the dangers of community notification laws outweigh the purpose they are designed to serve? Why or why not?

2. Louis J. Freeh provides statistics on the success of the "Innocent Images" program in which law enforcement agents identify child molesters on the Internet. Based on the program's success, he asks for increased authority to access encrypted communications, compile a DNA database and a national registry of sex offenders, and obtain subscriber names from Internet service providers to combat the exploitation of children on the Internet. Do you think the program's success justifies this authority? Does one type of authority seem more justified than another? Why or why not?

3. Observers such as Paul M. Rodriguez who want to ban computer-generated child pornography claim that child molesters cannot tell the difference between computer-generated and real child pornography. They reason, therefore, that if real child pornography encourages child molesters, then computer-generated images will do the same. Wendy Kaminer questions this logic because it is based on a presumption, not concrete evidence. Do you agree that the presumption is an insufficient reason to ban computer-generated child pornography? If so, what, if anything, would convince you that computer-generated child pornography should be banned?

Chapter 4

1. The National Coalition for Child Protection Reform contends that children should be with their biological parents and that family preservation programs have been successful at protecting children from further abuse. On the other hand, Susan Orr argues that some abusive parents can not be rehabilitated and that family preservation programs put their children at risk. Both provide evidence to support their conclusions. Which do you think is more convincing? Why?

2. Elizabeth Bartholet argues that strong adoption policies encouraging the adoption of children in foster care help abused children recover and heal. Dara Colwell, on the other hand, believes that policies favoring adoption can result in the unjustified termination of parental rights. Do you think policies that expedite the adoption of abused children placed in foster care infringe on parents' rights? Defend your answer citing evidence from the viewpoints.

3. Nadine Block cites research to support her argument that disciplinary spanking is child abuse and should therefore be banned. Okey Chigbo, however, questions the methodology and conclusions of antispanking research. He contends that spanking is not child abuse and is in some circumstances the only effective disciplinary tool available to parents. Do you agree with Chigbo's assessment of antispanking research? Why or why not?

Organizations to Contact

The editors have compiled the following list of organizations concerned with the issues debated in this book. The descriptions are derived from materials provided by the organizations. All have publications or information available for interested readers. The list was compiled on the date of publication of the present volume; names, addresses, phone and fax numbers, and e-mail and Internet addresses may change. Be aware that many organizations take several weeks or longer to respond to inquiries, so allow as much time as possible.

ACT for Kids
7 S. Howard, Suite 200, Spokane, WA 99201-3816
(866) 348-5437 • fax: (509) 747-0609
e-mail: resources@actforkids.org • website: www.actforkids.org

ACT for Kids is a nonprofit organization that provides resources, consultation, research, and training for the prevention and treatment of child abuse and sexual violence. The organization publishes workbooks, manuals, and books such as *He Told Me Not to Tell* and *How to Survive the Sexual Abuse of Your Child*.

American Academy of Child and Adolescent Psychiatry (AACAP)
3615 Wisconsin Ave. NW, Washington, DC 20016-3007
(202) 966-7300 • fax: (202) 966-2891
website: www.aacap.org

AACAP is a nonprofit organization that supports and advances child and adolescent psychiatry through research and the distribution of information. The academy's goal is to provide information that will remove the stigma associated with mental illnesses and assure proper treatment for children who suffer from mental or behavioral disorders due to child abuse, molestation, or other factors. AACAP publishes fact sheets on a variety of issues concerning disorders that may affect children and adolescents. Titles include "Child Sexual Abuse" and "Child Abuse—the Hidden Bruises."

American Bar Association (ABA)
Center on Children and the Law
740 15th St. NW, Washington, DC 20005
(202) 662-1720 • fax: (202) 662-1755
e-mail: ctrchildlaw@abanet.org • website: www.abanet.org/child

The ABA Center on Children and the Law aims to improve the quality of life for children through advances in law and public policy. It publishes the monthly *ABA Child Law Practice* and specialized information on legal matters related to the protection of children, including the book *Keeping Kids Out of the System*.

American Professional Society on the Abuse of Children (APSAC)

940 NE 13th St., Oklahoma City, OK 73104
(405) 271-8202 • fax: (405) 271-2931
e-mail: tricia-williams@ouhsc.edu • website: www.apsac.org

The APSAC is dedicated to improving the coordination of services in the fields of child abuse prevention, treatment, and research. It publishes a quarterly newsletter, the *Advisor*, and the *Journal of Interpersonal Violence*.

Center for Effective Discipline, Inc. (CED)

155 West Main St., Suite 1603, Columbus, OH 43215
(614) 221-8829 • fax: (614) 221-2110
e-mail: Infor@StopHitting.org • website: www.stophitting.org

The CED provides educational information to the public on the effects of corporal punishment of children and alternatives to its use and is the headquarters for End Physical Punishment of Children (EPOCH-USA). The center publishes guidelines for parents on its website, including "10 Guidelines for Raising a Well-Behaved Child."

Child Welfare League of America (CWLA)

440 First St. NW, Third Floor, Washington, DC 20001-2085
(202) 638-2952 • fax: (202) 638-4004
website: www.cwla.org

The Child Welfare League of America is an association of more than seven hundred public and private agencies and organizations devoted to improving the lives of children. CWLA publications include the book *Tender Mercies: Inside the World of a Child Abuse Investigator*, the quarterly magazine *Children's Voice*, and the bimonthly journal *Child Welfare*.

False Memory Syndrome Foundation

1955 Locust St., Philadelphia, PA 19103-5766
(215) 940-1040 • fax: (215) 940-1042
e-mail: mail@fmsfonline.org • website: www.fmsfonline.org

The foundation believes that many "delayed memories" of sexual abuse are the result of false memory syndrome (FMS). In FMS, patients in therapy "recall" childhood abuse that never occurred. The foundation seeks to discover reasons for the spread of FMS, works for the prevention of new cases, and aids FMS victims, including those falsely accused of abuse. The foundation publishes a newsletter and various papers and distributes articles and information on FMS.

Family Research Laboratory (FRL)

126 Horton Science Center, University of New Hampshire, Durham, NH 03824-3586
(603) 862-1888 • fax: (603) 862-1122
e-mail: murray.straus@unh.edu • website: www.unh.edu/frl

The FRL is an independent research group that studies the causes and consequences of family violence, including physical and sexual abuse of children and the connections between family violence and other social problems. A bibliography of works on these subjects, produced by staff members under the sponsorship of the University of New Hampshire, is available from the FRL, including *Corporal Punishment of Children in Theoretical Perspective*.

Family Violence and Sexual Assault Institute (FVSAI)

6160 Cornerstone Court East, San Diego, CA 92121
(858) 623-2777, ext. 406 • fax: (858) 646-0761
e-mail: fvsai@alliant.edu • website: www.fvsai.org

The FVSAI networks among people and agencies involved in studying, treating, protecting, or otherwise dealing with violent or abusive families. On its website, the FVSAI sponsors a book club that includes FVSAI's bibliographies, treatment manuals, and other books. Publications include the bibliographies *Sexual Abuse/Incest Survivors* and *Child Physical Abuse/Neglect*, and the quarterly *Family Violence and Sexual Assault Bulletin*.

Kempe Children's Center

1825 Marion St., Denver, CO 80218
(303) 864-5252 • fax: (303) 864-5302
e-mail: Kempe@KempeCenter.org
website: www.kempecenter.org

The Kempe Children's Center, formerly the C. Henry Kempe National Center for the Prevention and Treatment of Child Abuse and Neglect, is a resource for research on all forms of child abuse and neglect. It is committed to multidisciplinary approaches to improve recognition, treatment, and prevention of abuse. The center's resource library offers a catalog of books, booklets, information packets, and articles on child sexual abuse issues.

Klaas Kids Foundation
PO Box 925, Sausalito, CA 94966
(415) 331-6867 • fax: (415) 331-5633
e-mail: klaaskids@pacbell.net • website: www.klaaskids.org

The Klaas Kids Foundation was established in 1994 after the death of twelve-year-old kidnap and murder victim Polly Hannah Klaas. The foundation's goals are to acknowledge that crimes against children deserve a high priority and to form partnerships with concerned citizens, the private sector, organizations, law enforcement, and legislators to fight crimes against children. The foundation publishes a quarterly newsletter, the *Klaas Action Review*.

The Linkup
118 Chestnut St., Cloverport, KY 40111
(270) 788-6924
e-mail: ILINKUP@aol.com • website: www.thelinkup.com

The primary goal of the Linkup is to prevent clergy abuse and to empower and assist its victims to overcome its traumatic effects on their lives. The Linkup also encourages religious institutions to develop and implement responsible, accountable policies and procedures concerning sexual abuse. On its website, the *Missing Link Online*, The Linkup publishes news and articles.

National Association of State VOCAL Organizations (NASVO)
PO Box 1314, Orangevale, CA 95662
(800) 745-8778 • (916) 863-7470
website: www.nasvo.org

The National Association of State VOCAL (Victims of Child Abuse Laws) Organizations provides information and data, conducts research, and offers emotional support for those who have been falsely accused of child abuse. NASVO maintains a library of research on child abuse and neglect issues, focusing on legal, mental health, social, and medical issues, and will provide photocopies of articles for a fee. It publishes the bimonthly newsletter *NASVO News*.

National Center for Missing and Exploited Children (NCMEC)
699 Prince St., Alexandria, VA 22314
(800) THE LOST • (703) 739-0321
website: www.missingkids.com

The NCMEC serves as a clearinghouse of information on missing and exploited children and coordinates child protection efforts with the private sector. A number of publications on these issues are available, including guidelines for parents whose children are testifying in court and booklets such as *Child Molesters: A Behavioral Analysis* and *Child Pornography: It's a Crime*.

National Clearinghouse on Child Abuse and Neglect Information
330 C St. SW, Washington, DC 20447
(703) 385-7565 • (800) 394-3366 • fax: (703) 385-3206
e-mail: nccanch@calib.com • website: www.calib.com/nccanch

This national clearinghouse collects, catalogs, and disseminates information on all aspects of child maltreatment, including identification, prevention, treatment, public awareness, training, and education. The clearinghouse offers various reports, fact sheets, and bulletins concerning child abuse and neglect.

National Criminal Justice Reference Service (NCJRS)
PO Box 6000, Rockville, MD 20849-6000
(301) 519-5500 • (800) 851-3420 • fax: (301) 519-5212
e-mail: askncjrs@ncjrs.org • website: www.ncjrs.org

NCJRS is a research and development agency of the U.S. Department of Justice established to prevent and reduce crime and to improve the criminal justice system. Among its publications are *Permanency Planning for Abused and Neglected Children* and *When Your Child Is Missing: A Family Survival Guide*.

National District Attorneys Association
American Prosecutors Research Institute
National Center for Prosecution of Child Abuse
99 Canal Center Plaza, Suite 510, Alexandria, VA 22314
(703) 549-9222 • fax: (703) 836-3195
e-mail: ncpca@ndaa-apri.org
website: www.ndaa-apri.org/apri/programs/ncpca/index.html

The National Center for Prosecution of Child abuse seeks to improve the investigation and prosecution of child abuse cases. A clearinghouse on child abuse laws and court reforms, the center supports research on reducing courtroom trauma for child victims. It publishes a monthly newsletter, *Update*, as well as monographs, bibliographies, special reports, and a manual for prosecutors, *Investigation and Prosecution of Child Abuse*.

Safer Society Foundation
PO Box 340-1, Brandon, VT 05733-0340
(802) 247-3132 • fax: (802) 247-4233
website: www.safersociety.org

The Safer Society Foundation is a national research, advocacy, and referral center for the prevention of sexual abuse of children and adults. The Safer Society Press publishes studies and books on treatment for sexual abuse victims and offenders and on the prevention of sexual abuse, including *Fuel on the Fire: An Inquiry into "Pornography" and Sexual Aggression in a Free Society.*

Survivors Network of Those Abused by Priests (SNAP)
PO Box 6416, Chicago, IL 60680
(312) 409-2720
e-mail: SNAPBlaine@hotmail.com
website: www.peak.org/~snapper

SNAP provides support for men and women who were sexually abused by any member of the clergy, including priests, brothers, nuns, deacons, and teachers. The network provides an extensive phone network, advocacy, information, and referrals. On its website, SNAP provides access to a discussion board, news, and information on legal issues.

VOICES in Action, Inc.
PO Box 13, Newtonsville, OH 45158
(800) 786-4238
e-mail: voicesinaction@aol.com • website: www.voices-action.org

Victims of Incest Can Emerge Survivors (VOICES) provides assistance to victims of incest and child sexual abuse and promotes awareness about the prevalence of incest. It publishes a bibliography and the newsletter the *Chorus.* On its website, VOICES provides a reading list and links to purchase books on incest and child sexual abuse.

Bibliography of Books

Amnesty International *Hidden Scandal, Secret Shame: Torture and Ill-Treatment of Children.* New York: Amnesty International Publications, 2000.

Carlos A. Arnaldo, ed. *Child Abuse on the Internet: Ending the Silence.* New York: Berghahn Books, 2001.

Leory Ashby *Endangered Children: Dependency, Neglect, and Abuse in American History.* New York: Macmillan, 1997.

Elizabeth Bartholet *Nobody's Children: Abuse and Neglect, Foster Drift, and the Adoption Alternative.* Boston: Beacon, 1999.

Rebecca Morris Bolen *Child Sexual Abuse: Its Scope and Our Failure.* New York: Kluwer Academic/Plenum, 2001.

John Briere, Lucy Berliner, and Josephine A. Bulkey, eds. *The ASPAC Handbook on Child Maltreatment.* Newbury Park, CA: Sage, 2000.

Terence W. Campbell *Smoke and Mirrors: The Devastating Effect of False Sexual Abuse Claims.* New York: Insight, 1998.

Robin E. Clark *The Encyclopedia of Child Abuse*, 2nd ed. New York: Facts On File, 2001.

Cynthia Crosson-Tower *Understanding Child Abuse and Neglect.* Boston: Allyn and Bacon, 1999.

Tracee De Hahn *Crimes Against Children: Child Abuse and Neglect.* Philadelphia: Chelsea House, 2000.

Margie Druss Fodor *Megan's Law: Protection or Privacy?* Berkeley Heights, NJ: Enslow, 2001.

Richard B. Gartner *Betrayed as Boys: Psychodynamic Treatment of Sexually Abused Men.* New York: Guilford, 1999.

Kathlyn Gay *Child Labor: A Global Crisis.* Brookfield, CT: Millbrook, 1998.

Healing Woman Foundation *The Healing Journal: The International Journal for Survivors of Childhood Sexual Abuse.* Baltimore: Sidran, 2002.

Mary Edna Helfer, Ruth S. Kempe, and Richard D. Krugman, eds. *The Battered Child.* Chicago: University of Chicago Press, 1999.

Sandra K. Hewitt *Assessing Allegations of Sexual Abuse in Preschool Children: Understanding Small Voices.* Newbury Park, CA: Sage, 2000.

Philip Jenkins	*Beyond Tolerance: Child Pornography on the Internet.* New York: New York University Press, 2001.
Philip Jenkins	*Moral Panic: Changing Concepts of the Child Molester in Modern America.* New Haven, CT: Yale University Press, 1998.
Philip Jenkins	*Pedophiles and Priests: Anatomy of a Contemporary Crisis.* New York: Oxford University Press, 1996.
Robin Karr-Morse, Meredith S. Wiley, and T. Berry Brazelton	*Ghosts from the Nursery: Tracing the Roots of Violence.* New York: Grove/Atlantic, 1999.
Eugene C. Kennedy	*The Unhealed Wound: The Church and Human Sexuality.* New York: St. Martin's, 2001.
James R. Kincaid	*Erotic Innocence: The Culture of Child Molesting.* Durham, NC: Duke University Press, 1998.
John R. Lutzker, ed.	*Handbook of Child Abuse Research and Treatment.* New York: Plenum, 1998.
Sara Markowitz	*Alcohol Regulation and Violence Towards Children.* Cambridge, MA: National Bureau of Economic Research, 1998.
Anna J. Michener	*Becoming Anna: The Autobiography of a Sixteen-Year-Old.* Chicago: University of Chicago Press, 1998.
Nancy J. Napier	*Getting Through the Day: Strategies for Adults Hurt as Children.* Baltimore: Sidran, 2002.
Christina Paxson	*Work, Welfare, and Child Maltreatment.* Cambridge, MA: National Bureau of Economic Research, 1999.
Ronald T. Potter-Efron and Patricia S. Potter-Efron, eds.	*Aggression, Family Violence, and Chemical Dependency.* Binghamton, NY: Haworth, 1996.
Cara Elizabeth Richards	*The Loss of Innocents: Child Killers and Their Victims.* Wilmington, DE: Scholarly Resources, 2000.
Keith N. Richards	*Tender Mercies: Inside the World of a Child Abuse Investigator.* Washington, DC: Child Welfare League of America, 1999.
Diana E.H. Russell	*The Epidemic of Rape and Child Sexual Abuse in the United States.* Thousand Oaks, CA: Sage, 2000.
Andren Schoen and Brian Prats	*Beyond the Big Easy: One Man's Triumph over Abuse.* Tempe, AZ: New Falcon, 2000.

Beth M. Schwartz-Kenney, Michelle McCauley, and Michelle A. Epstein, eds.	*Child Abuse: A Global View.* Westport, CT: Greenwood, 2001.
Eric Shelman and Stephen Lazoritz	*Out of the Darkness: The Story of Mary Ellen Wilson.* Lake Forest, CA: Dolphin Moon Publishing, 1999.
Sue William Silverman	*Because I Remember Terror, Father, I Remember You.* Athens: University of Georgia Press, 1999.
Murray A. Straus	*Beating the Devil Out of Them: Corporal Punishment in American Families and Its Effects on Children.* New Brunswick, NJ: Transaction Publishers, 2001.
Susan M. Turner	*Something to Cry About: An Argument Against Corporal Punishment of Children in Canada.* Waterloo, ON: Wilfrid Lauier University Press, 2002.
Jane Waldfogel	*The Future of Child Protection: How to Break the Cycle of Abuse and Neglect.* Cambridge, MA: Harvard University Press, 1998.
Vernon Wiehe	*Sibling Abuse: Hidden Physical, Emotional, and Sexual Trauma.* Thousand Oaks, CA: Sage, 1997.

Index

217

child pornography and, 45
homosexuality and, 90, 101–103
Internet use and, 52–53, 54
media's sexualized images of children
   and, 17, 47
national register of convicted, 55–56
sex tourism and, 49
see also community notification laws;
   priests, sexual abuse by; sex
   offenders; sexual abuse
pedophilia
   as a complex sexual disorder, 102
   misconceptions of, 62
Pelton, Leroy, 27
Peterson, David, 195
Pixley, Latrena, 158
Plante, Wendy A., 198
police. *See* law enforcement
pornography. *See* child pornography
   (Internet)
Porter, James, 68
poverty
   associated with child abuse, 27, 29
   examples of child abuse and neglect
      cases due to, 28–30
   as most frequently noted risk for
      child abuse, 22
   neglect and, 27–28
pregnancy, drug use during, 35,
   165–66
priests, sexual abuse by
   American Catholics on, 74
   as betraying trust of Catholic
      families, 77–79
   celibacy and, 63, 87, 95–97
   church's excuses for, 71–72
   church's knowledge of, 59–60, 72, 86
   church's response to, 60
      bishop reporting requirements and,
         65–67
      protecting image of the church
         and, 72–73, 86
      suggested, 103–104
      as varying, 100–101
   danger of simplistic solutions to,
      83–84
   death of medieval church and, 73–74
   evaluating assumptions on, 63–64
   homosexuality and, 64–65, 83,
      87–93, 101–103
   incidences of, 59
   percentage of, 66
   re-offenders, 67–68
   restoring credibility in the church
      after, 75
   Vatican meeting on, 60, 82
   zero-tolerance policy for
      bishops role in, 81–83

as leading to future abuses, 81
   risks of, 68–69
   support for, 77, 78, 79
privacy rights, 112, 118–19, 132
Proctor, Gary, 179

Ramsey, JonBenet, 16
Ravenel, S. DuBose, 196
Reardon, Christopher, 88
Reid, Caprice, 14
research
   on abuse of children with disabilities,
      39–41
   on intervention strategies, 23–24
   on sexual abuse of children, 99–101
   on spanking, 186–87, 196–98
Rich, Frank, 17
Riley, Linda, 176
Robertshaw, Corinne, 194, 195
Rodriguez, Paul M., 138
Rooney, Don, 59
Rosemond, John, 199–200
Rossetti, Stephen J., 61
Rossi, Peter, 160–61
Runnion, Samantha, 45

Saffran, Dennis, 160
Sagendorf, Thomas E., 184
Saunders, Bernadette J., 13
Scalia, Antonin, 146
Scholle, Alan D., 113
Schroeder, Elizabeth, 118
Schurink, Evanthe, 12–13
sex offenders
   DNA profiles of, 125–26
   employment and, 113–14
   recidivism rates of, 140
   registration of, 113, 126–27
   undercover investigation for online,
      123–24
   violence and vigilantism against,
      117–18
   see also community notification laws;
      pedophiles; priests, sexual abuse by;
      sexual abuse
sex tourism, 49–52, 55
sexual abuse
   celibacy in the priesthood and, 87,
      95, 97
   child pornography encourages, 141
      con, 144–45
   child prostitution, 49–52
   of children with disabilities, 43
   in foster care, 153–54
   homosexuality and, 88
   impact of public notification laws on,
      120
   international cooperation for law